A Time Traveler's Commencement

A Time Traveler's Commencement

Stanton Call

Yazdan Publishing

A Time Traveler's Commencement

Yazdan Publishing First Printing, November 2022

Printed in the United States of America

ISBN-13: 978-1-938838-15-6

Yazdan Publishing
P O Box 56545
Virginia Beach, VA 23456

*To all who have had occasion to glimpse
beyond the illusion of space and time . . .*

and in appreciation of George Peabody (1795-1869),
Manuela Sáenz (1797-1856),
Emanuel Swedenborg (1688-1772),
and Marie Louise Habets (1905-1986)
for their ongoing part in the tale.

It is a certainty that while I lived my travels were regarded as substantial. Since the occasion of my death and my recruitment into the League, however, these journeys have expanded far beyond anything I might have previously imagined. Over the course of my employment, I have found occasion to undertake voyages to more periods in history than might be readily called to mind and no less than six of the seven continents. (To be sure, there appears little need for my labors in Antarctica.)

I am one of those charged with ensuring that the approved timeline (ATL) remains intact and rectified at every point along the way. Although it is uncertain how long this task might be ours to undertake, we have been employed for this purpose and this purpose alone. Whether the pursuit of this engagement ends tomorrow or should persist for a thousand years remains unknown to me. Such is the fate of all Time Travelers in service to the League and the Core which governs it.

Ben #239, recruit

As a recruit, two purposes will shine as a beacon ever before you. The first is a commitment to the League and the ongoing preservation of the ATL contained within the Akasha. The second is your allegiance to ensuring consciousness growth for the Whole of humankind. As long as these two goals are held ever in mind, your efforts will not be in vain.

To be sure, from the illusory perspective of space-time, all too frequently these goals may appear distant and even beyond your control. When that occurs, however, know that this has been the very experience of so many others before you — ever since Moment One first entered the collective consciousness. Be not discouraged by the inevitable. Just as it is inevitable that these thoughts will come to you, without doubt, our ultimate success remains a certainty.

Excerpt, "Introduction Orientation," *A Time Traveler's Code of Conduct* **by Ruth #7**

ONE: *Journal Entry — October 14 ATL*

I am a Time Traveler. According to the reckoning of the approved timeline (ATL), such has been my position for nigh unto seven months now. To be sure much has occurred since my arrival and the activities that demand my attention have rarely given me adequate pause to truly have occasion to ponder the trade with which I now find myself involved, let alone provide sufficient attention to all of the undertakings requiring my personal resolution and focus. I have Agnes's school curriculum to contend with, the ongoing rigors of my travels, too few alliances with my sweetheart Athena (as we both remain quite occupied with matters of the League), and the frequent interactions and discussions with my classmates, my roomie George among them. I should note herein that although the school's records continue to designate George as my official roommate, whenever the occasion presents itself, I find myself lodging within Athena's chambers for what we called in my day the "shaking of the sheets."

As far as the school curriculum is concerned, as of late, Agnes #23 has become even more intense in her ongoing role as instructress. Whether this is due to the fact that graduation and our forthcoming commencement into the field as full-fledged Wayfarers is less than eight weeks hence or because the Governor-General herself, Sara #11, has suggested that changes will be coming to the Core which oversees the League school remains unclear to me. What is certain is that the pace of the curriculum has not abated and the immensity of the "required final exam" that Agnes seems fond of calling to mind at every opportunity grows larger in scope with her every mention of it.

As I surmised from the very beginning of my recruitment, there is sufficient work to keep us all industrious and constantly occupied with this business of time travel. My forte continues to be those missions that focus on the need for some measure of diplomacy. I should note, however, that ever since Emmett deserted the League for his own selfish pursuits, prompting Athena's promotion to his former post as "Keeper of the Records" for the Akasha Library, mission assignments have not always come to us as organized as they had previously. It is apparent that Athena's prior efforts within the ATL Mission Office had provided both order and structure, and Milton #71 as mission supervisor needs to find an assistant as quickly as possible to help him with the ongoing responsibilities of these time traveling matters. Whether someone from "out in the field" (as Agnes refers to Time Travelers employed beyond the headquarters facility) or one of my own classmates will apply for this post remains unknown to me. Certainly, it has not been a primary focus of conversation during any of our discussions within the League Café.

Between the demands of the curriculum, our frequent time travel assignments, a never-ending list of homework assignments, and my desire to maintain some semblance of camaraderie with my classmates, I strive to find any possible occasion to court and woo Athena, my Mediterranean lass. Our affection for one another has not abated. In spite of our familiarity with one another, I continue to be drawn to her smile, the intensity of her brown eyes, her amazing intellect on so many topics of import, and the way she curls her hair around a fingertip whenever deep in conversation or thought.

Next to Athena, my roomie, George #111, remains my closest friend and confidant. To be sure, in spite of the ongoing curriculum verifying the nature of time as ultimately possessing only NOW with its infinite manifestations, George possesses both a kind heart and the mind of a banker, as he has not lost a fondness for either linear thought or ciphering. Whereas matters of diplomacy remain my primary focus on these mission assignments, George finds himself ever involved in philanthropy and giving assistance to those unfortunate who have had hardship thrust upon them.

In a similar manner, our dark-haired Latin classmate, Manuela #64, has found her niche as a frequent champion of those who deserve some measure of dignity and equality. Her assignments have repeatedly

placed her within positions of influence enabling her to
serve in a variety of capacities, such as a guardian for
child laborers, an advocate for the rights of women, a
champion for the underpaid, a defender of democracy
(and the capacity to vote within same), and a promoter
of all manner of social change.

Her French roomie, Bonne Soeur Marie #304,
continues to focus on those time-traveling matters that
generally deal with healing, medicine, and every manner
of health and wellbeing for the body, mind, and spirit.
I have come to believe that her gift for all manner of
therapeutic and curative measures is truly remarkable.

Obviously, as it relates to matters of the spirit, our
attentive Swede, Emanuel #41, has found himself
something of a spiritual liberator and continues
to specialize in missions pertaining to religion,
faith, transcendence, and all matters of personal
enlightenment.

As has oft been our usual morning routine, we five
find ourselves sitting in class with Agnes #23 standing
at the ready, stylus in hand which she waved before
us even as she began the scheduled curriculum for the
day. "We are going to examine another amazing case
history!" Agnes said excitedly as she bounced about
before the classroom, assuring us as she had on so many
other occasions: "This is truly an incredible story!"

George #111 turned toward me and mouthed the
words, "Background information," as such always
proceeded one of her tales.

As I gazed upon our instructress, I could not help but
notice that her dark-skinned face appeared to be glowing,
as though she had recently undergone some manner of
rigorous facial. It quickly became apparent that some
quantity of makeup had been applied to highlight the
curvature of her eyes. Before I had managed to surmise

the cause of such a change in her appearance, it was Manuela #64 who inquired aloud:

"Are you going on a date, Ms. Agnes?"

"What?!" Agnes seemed startled, even horrified that some tremendous secret had suddenly been divulged to the class. It took a moment to regain her composure before assuring us, "I am simply trying to look my best."

"Pourquoi . . . Why?" came the query from Bonne Soeur Marie.

"It is of no matter," she said quickly. She glanced upon the looks of curiosity on each of the faces before her and added, "If you must know, my friend from the old days, Nashwa #86, will be coming for a visit any day now. Can we get back to the coursework?"

Our teacher shook her head in frustration and turned to the whiteboard behind her to write the words "Hamburg Bombing Time Slip" with the stylus, taking occasion to underline them twice over for emphasis.

"We will explore the Hamburg bombing time slip." As the name was spoken, she peered intensely upon each of us as a means of adding an additional measure of significance to the tale. "The evidence that time is not a constant is absolutely overwhelming. This is just one more example of how those crippled by the Collective Illusion of space-time could see beyond their limitations if they would simply choose to look!"

Agnes pointed the stylus at each student, in turn, reminding the five of us, "This incident will be on the required final exam, so you need to pay attention! It occurred in the Collective Illusion of the 20th century and was witnessed by two individuals, co-workers employed by the city's oldest newspaper, *Hamburgischer Korrespondent*. This took place within the ATL of 1932, when the paper sent J. Bernard Hutton as a reporter and Joachim Brandt to accompany him as a photographer.

Now some important background information you will
need to know is that for a long while Britain led the
world in shipbuilding . . ."

As she turned to the whiteboard and wrote the word
"shipyard" with her stylus, George turned to me and
whispered, "Told you."

She continued, "Even during much of the 19th
century, many German companies bought their ships
directly from the British. That began to change in the late
1880s so that by the time the Great War came around,
Germany was building its own ships and the largest
shipbuilder was Blohm & Voss. They had an amazing
shipyard facility and built all kinds of ships—civilian
craft, sailing vessels of every imaginable size, and steel-
hulled warships, including the Bismarck. Those are the
basics!" Agnes slapped her free hand on the top of her
desk for emphasis, as well as to guarantee that we five
were listening.

Her tale resumed, "Hutton and Brandt had been
assigned to tour the shipyard in order to provide the
paper's readers with a timeline and photographic
documentation of the industry's growth. You know,
Blohm & Voss was a major employer for the city." As was
her method of providing some semblance of theatrical
component to her presentations, she began to pace
about before us. For a time, she appeared to look upon
every corner of the classroom, illustrating the activity of
touring the shipyard facility. Her act of walking before
us continued for a time until Agnes presumed that her
demonstration of such a tour was sufficient for our
comprehension, at which point she added, "This was
one year before the Nazis rose to power—a time when
the shipyard would experience even greater growth—
but it was still an amazing facility. They were taken
everywhere. By the end of their visit, they had toured

the entire shipyard. The two were certain they had enough material for a great feature story."

Agnes stopped moving about, informing us, "What happened next was truly amazing! As the two started walking toward the car, which they had left just beyond the shipyard gates, they suddenly heard the sounds of dozens of aircraft engines flying overhead. As they looked up, they could see the sky had filled with fighter planes but they weren't German. British bombers from the Royal Airforce were descending upon the shipyard!" Our teacher took a moment to stare toward the ceiling and then moved her arms apart to demonstrate the appearance of flight by traveling halfway around the desk. Suddenly, she stared in horror at the ceiling and continued her narrative.

"Bombs fell from the sky just as the anti-aircraft artillery upon the ground began firing. They heard massive explosions and could see fires breaking out with the impact of every shell. Buildings began to collapse. Ships upon the waterfront were continually struck by British fighters. Quickly, Brandt took his camera and began to take pictures of the fighter planes above, the destruction of the bombs upon the ground, and more than a dozen shots of the chaos that ensued as men ran for their lives."

Agnes proceeded to take imaginary photographs of the scene she had just described. "When he had finished, the two hurried toward the gates, passing a security guard who encouraged them to leave immediately. The sounds of death, destruction, and confusion were everywhere. Even as they drove from the shipyard, they could hear the ongoing sounds of the attack."

Suddenly, the stylus was shaken before us while Agnes noted aloud, "The two had driven about a block when all at once the sky grew clear. The sounds of the fighter planes were completely silenced and everything in the city of Hamburg suddenly appeared calm and normal. They stopped the car and got out to look at the shipyard behind them. What they saw came as quite a shock for there were no fighter planes, no bombs, no destruction, no flames, nothing out of the ordinary! The shipyard appeared just the same as it had when they first entered the gates. Not knowing what else to do, the two hurried to the newspaper office to describe the scene they had just witnessed. No one believed them. Brandt decided to get the pictures he had taken as evidence of the attack but when the photographs were developed they contained only images of a clear sky, a bustling shipyard, and countless 'riggers' working throughout the facility . . . riggers, that's the word for some of the shipyard employees," Agnes wrote the word upon the board.

"Both Hutton and Brandt insisted they had seen something. They were so adamant they were telling the truth that the newspaper editor finally called the shipyard manager who informed him that absolutely nothing unusual had occurred that day. Now, it is somewhat unclear whether the two were fired or simply quit their jobs due to the heckling of their coworkers. Brandt found another job as a photographer within the city, and before the breakout of World War II, Hutton had moved to England."

Agnes paused for only a moment before assuring us, "But that is not the end of the story! Eleven years later, during the final week of July 1943, British papers carried a headline about a massive bombing attack that had just occurred within Hamburg, its oil refineries, and the shipyard. It was an extended campaign that virtually destroyed the entire city, killed 37,000 civilians, and wounded more than 180,000 people. On the front page was a picture of the bombed shipyard, just as Hutton and Brandt had seen it firsthand back in 1932! That is the Hamburg bombing time slip."

Agnes stopped speaking and looked out at her students. "For extra credit," she said enthusiastically, "who can tell me why England gave this attack the code name 'Operation Gomorrah?'"

At the same moment, George #111 and Emanuel #41 each waved an arm into the air, seeking to be called upon. Agnes pointed to Emanuel and stated, "Last time, I let George answer first."

"Madame Agnes," my Swede classmate spoke with certainty, "I would imagine it is simply a reference to the story contained in Genesis in which the Canaanite cities of Sodom and Gomorrah are destroyed by fire and brimstone from the air."

"Exactly!" Agnes declared in agreement, before adding, "You know, for as long as he lived J. Bernard Hutton told others about his experience with Brandt there in Hamburg. Eventually, his story was picked up and even became part of a children's book—imagine a children's book! The title was *The Little Giant Book of Eerie Thrills & Unspeakable Chills*, but few individuals ever became aware of this story or understood that it was a historical event!" Agnes shook her head in disgust.

Before she could say another word, the classroom door flew open and the Governor-General, Sara #11, entered the room; Milton #71 stood by her side.

Sara's voice was somber, "I need you all to come to the Akasha Library. I have just called a special meeting of the entire facility. We may have discovered a major problem."

"What is it?" Agnes #23 appeared alarmed.

The Governor-General sighed aloud words that she never imagined might fall from her lips, "It appears someone may be creating an alternate ATL."

"I cannot imagine how such a thing is even possible!" Agnes muttered to herself as we all headed down the various passageways and corridors leading to the library. Our teacher followed Sara and Milton through one hallway after another, while the five of us trailed close behind. She continued to chatter to herself, declaring loud enough for us all to hear, "Who could be doing such a thing?" and, "This is only going to add complications to our work!" and, "Whoever is responsible should be eradicated immediately!"

As the League building was vast in size, it took some measure of time to reach the library facility, traveling through one corridor and then another until we finally arrived at the enormous double doorway. Milton pulled open one door while Sara opened the other, and we were quickly ushered inside the massive chambers. The expanse was filled with an endless supply of hundreds of thousands of books that had been organized on countless shelves rising several stories above the ground. We followed Sara and Milton to the center of the room, where the book stacks fanned out in every direction. A large whiteboard had been rolled into place and more than 20 chairs had been placed in front of the board; most of which were already filled with League employees, including three additional members of the Core: Grimwald #94 (our Elder Professor); Emma #119, whose black-rimmed spectacles gave her a constant look of severity; and the ever-youthful Ruth #7, my personal recruiter and the beloved author of our text.

I saw Athena #56 sitting in the front row but as

others had already occupied the chairs on either side of her, George #111 and I walked toward two empty seats next to each other. After taking our place, he turned to me and whispered, "Isn't Emma supposed to be on probation for spying on other Core members?"

I responded quickly, "Yes, the investigation is ongoing."

The last person to arrive for the meeting was a member of the café staff at which point the Governor-General began.

"Thank you for joining us." The words which followed sounded serious, "I do not fully understand the ramifications of what you are about to hear, but I have asked our League historian and ATL Mission Supervisor, Milton #71, to tell you what he told me earlier today. Milton?"

Milton rose and came forward, while Sara moved toward an available chair. He stood for a moment near the whiteboard and looked out upon each of us. Although I had often found occasion to appreciate his English accent and cheery disposition, on this occasion his words were filled with concern.

"What I am about to tell you has troubled me greatly. This could have major ramifications for the League and for each and every one of you. It was something I came across quite by accident, and when I found it, I thought it imperative to confer with Athena. I am somewhat uncertain how to tell you this . . ."

Emma #119 shook her head in frustration, peered at him over her spectacles, and impatiently interrupted, "Just tell us what you saw!"

Milton nodded and took a stylus in hand from the tray beneath the whiteboard, "I think it might be easiest to explain it with a diagram." Halfway up the board, he drew a black, straight-line from one end of the whiteboard to the other. "Let us imagine that this line is the ATL, the approved timeline that the Core has authorized and the League works to maintain."

Once the line was in place, he took a blue stylus and appeared to be drawing various lines that intersected the straight line from every direction. From one end of the black line to the other, he used the blue stylus to repeatedly cross and recross the black line representing the ATL.

"Let us imagine that these blue lines represent various timelines in opposition to the approved timeline. These oppositions are essentially the timelines we constantly rectify in our work, managing time as it should be. As you know, when something is out of alignment with the approved timeline and threatens to vie for prominence, the Akasha system notifies us immediately. As you have all heard repeatedly, a major misalignment prompts the emergency alarm system throughout the entire facility and a swift response from the ATL Mission Office, which selects specific Time Travelers to correct the problem."

"I hate that damn bell!" one of the café employees voiced aloud.

Milton nodded in agreement and then took a red stylus and carefully drew it for several inches exactly on top of a portion of the black line, "Let us imagine this red line indicates something in complete accord with the ATL. As we all understand, whenever anything is in complete accord with the approved timeline it goes unnoticed; there is no reason for the system to notify the League because time is in accord with what has been approved by the Core. Is everyone with me so far?"

Although only silence greeted his question, several heads nodded in the affirmative.

Milton #71 resumed his dialogue, "Yesterday afternoon I was looking into the Akasha Library for some preliminary background information on Aristotle and his system of logical reasoning that has come to be called 'syllogism' . . ."

Immediately, Bonne Soeur Marie #304 interrupted, raising a hand over her head and inquiring, "Qu'est-ce que c'est, Monsieur? What is that?"

"It is a system of deduction in which a conclusion can often be ascertained from two related premises." Milton paused for only a moment as a means of formulating an example, "If I were to say, 'All students at the League are Time Travelers,' and then I was to inform you, 'Bonne Soeur Marie is a student at the League,' it is logical for us to conclude that 'Bonne Soeur Marie is a Time Traveler.' That is the reasoning proposed by Aristotle's system of syllogism."

Milton continued, "In any event, while I was researching Aristotle, I came across what I can only describe as a shadow of a timeline. It was there, and I could see it—but rather than appearing like a normal timeline, it was somewhat ephemeral. It had the appearance of an outline or a faint reflection of the real timeline. What I saw dealt with Alexander the Great, one of Aristotle's students. Because it was so unusual in appearance, I brought it immediately to Athena's attention."

Agnes #23 volunteered aloud from her seat, "Athena knows everything!" while nodding in the affirmative.

Milton concurred, "Yes, I thought Athena was the best one to verify what I had seen and Athena saw it as well—a partially formed shadow of an alternate timeline existing within the Akasha. For a few moments, we both watched what appeared to be another timeline in complete alignment with the ATL. In the next instant, it was gone."

My roomie, George, voiced aloud the very question

that had come to my mind, "What do you think it means?"

"I do not want to create any unnecessary alarm," Milton was quick to respond, "but it would appear that someone is attempting to create a duplicate ATL timeline—an alternate history from the one approved by the Core."

I chose to speak, "To what end?"

Milton looked toward the Governor-General, who rose to respond to my query.

"Ben," she began gravely, "if someone has managed to create a portion of an alternate ATL, I imagine it would be beyond any of the controls that the Core has in place. Once that was accomplished, virtually anything might occur within this alternate timeline beyond either our notice or oversight."

My roomie waved a hand in the air and then inquired aloud, "How is this even possible? How could someone create a duplicate of the approved timeline?"

Sara #11 pointed toward Ruth #7 and invited her to respond, "Ruth, can you tell everyone what you told me?"

Ruth nodded, stood, and turned to reply, "It would be possible if someone began with a lesser timeline that was almost identical to the ATL. That individual could use the influence of one or more Wayfarers to repeatedly alter the lesser timeline ever so slightly until it became an exact duplicate of the approved timeline."

"What timeline is being altered?" I added, "The ATL Mission Office can send one of us to stop whatever is happening."

Ruth was quick to explain, "Ben, because the timeline is identical to our own, we have no way of knowing which one is being altered. A duplicate will completely bypass all of the systems we have in place."

Elder Professor Grimwald #94 ruminated aloud, "I assume you have all given thought to the reason Alexander the Great is the intended target?" The expression on his kind, dark face turned to one of concern.

"We have," Sara responded immediately.

It was my classmate Manuela #64 who interrupted, "Why would Alexander the Great be the target?"

As Core historian, Milton #71 appeared most qualified to respond, "Because it was Alexander who pulled together the largest empire that the ancient world has ever known."

Silence filled the room for only a moment before I chose to ask a question for which I believed I already possessed the answer, "Have you given thought to who might be capable of creating such an alternate timeline?"

Both Milton and Sara nodded in the affirmative but it was the Governor-General herself who spoke the name aloud, "Emmett, our former Keeper of the Records."

The meeting concluded with Sara #11 indicating that she had called an emergency gathering of all Core members currently within the facility. (By my own count, that equated to five of the nine: Sara, Milton, Emma, Grimwald, and Ruth being present, whereas Hina, Hakim, Lucius, and Mia were apparently elsewhere in the field.) Completely forgetting my desire to speak with Athena and confirm our plans for the evening, I followed my roomie out into the hallway. It was George who spoke first.

"Emmett is a traitor," he said with some measure of frustration. "There is no way to ascertain what he might be attempting by creating an alternate ATL."

I sighed in response, "Perhaps he is simply moving forward on what he was unable to do on the timeline with Elizabeth I?"

George was quick and to the point, "You are still too fond of him. He is much more dangerous than you may be ready to believe."

"What are you thinking?" I asked.

"Emmett has been involved in this work for eons . . . as time is measured beyond this facility," George quickly added. "He helped create the entire League program. He recruited many of those who call themselves Wayfarers. We can't possibly imagine all the knowledge he already possesses or how he might use that knowledge against the League."

I nodded reluctantly, stating that which came to mind, "Later tonight, I will ask Athena for her thoughts on the matter." At the mention of her name, I remembered, "Athena! I forgot to talk to her about tonight."

"Tell your girlfriend I said 'Hi,'" George responded, as I turned and hurried back toward the library's entrance.

Although I had long strived to overcome my habit of running through the hallways and corridors of the League facility, I nearly bumped into Emma #119, as I entered the library doors just as she was leaving. She peered over her black-rimmed spectacles, looked me straight in the eyes, and made her displeasure known, "There is something very wrong with you, young man."

Even though I was still unused to being called "young man," I chose to apologize and allowed her to pass without further comment on my part. Once she had departed, I hurried toward the center of the chamber.

It became immediately clear that Athena was gone and everyone else had left or was walking down one of the library's many book corridors, I found Ruth #7 sitting by herself, staring at the whiteboard before her. She appeared troubled, prompting me to take the seat next to her.

"You look worried."

Her comely face turned toward me. Although she chose the appearance of a 20-year-old, I had once seen her as an elderly woman during the occasion of her own recruitment. Regardless of her age, however, her eyes sparkled with vigor.

"I am concerned that we may be facing a much bigger problem than we have yet to imagine," she said assuredly.

"What kind of problem?"

"You understand that much of our work occurs because the Akasha becomes aware of various timelines vying for prominence with the ATL?"

"Absolutely!"

"And do you remember the words from the classroom text dealing with revisiting the same timeline more than once?"

"I believe so," I said, before responding with a quote from the very text she had written, "'Once interaction with a timeline has occurred, space-time is altered ever so slightly.'"

"That's right," Ruth nodded in agreement. "I am concerned that Emmett's creation of an alternate timeline may have ramifications that even he has yet to consider."

"I imagine you are more informed regarding what might be possible than anyone else here."

She nodded a second time, "Although it is problematic and will definitely add many complications to our work, Emmett's creation of an alternate ATL is not my greatest concern. I am certain that he and anyone else he has gathered — Wayfarers who have abandoned this work — will dabble for a time in the creation of whatever history they might choose to create. However, once they have grown tired of such foolishness we may face a much bigger threat."

The tone of her words alarmed me, "What kind of threat?"

"Given enough energy and thought, Emmett's alternate timeline may vie for prominence over the ATL, and if that occurs, two things will become very possible."

"I'm listening."

"Because space-time becomes altered with every revisitation of the same moment in time, Emmett or any of his followers would have the ability to leave one instant in the Collective Illusion on their alternate timeline and come to the very same period on the approved timeline authorized by the Core, prompting changes over which we would have no control . . ."

I could not help but interrupt, "Nor would we possess any memory that such a change had even occurred?"

"That's correct."

"And what is the second possibility?"

"I cannot be certain if it has yet to enter Emmett's mind but I believe it would be possible for someone to bring an individual from that alternate timeline to the ATL — a duplicate. If that occurs, there is no reason why that duplicate could not eventually arrive at the League facility. Perhaps Emmett could recruit a duplicate you, or a duplicate me, or a duplicate Governor-General, or a duplicate of anyone else." She sighed before adding, "They could then choose to eradicate whomever they decided from the real ATL, allowing the substitute to remain as a replacement."

The thought was alarming, but I managed to inquire, "And no one would ever know?"

Ruth nodded for a third time, "No one would ever know."

When Moment One gave birth to the illusion of space-time, everything was altered, forever changed from the consciousness of Oneness that had previously existed. Before the inception of space-time, there was only harmony — harmony of thought and harmony of purpose. The result which occurred thereafter became one of dissension, disagreement, disorder, and a disregard for what had once been true. Your mission as a Time Traveler is to not only rectify the timeline but to aid in the reawakening of the very consciousness that once guided all of Creation to be Whole.

Beyond that, the existence of countless timelines vying for their own prominence will complicate your efforts. Every choice and every decision of each individual will continue to possess the potential to manipulate the timeline outside the parameters condoned by the ATL. All this will simply be part of your training and a growing understanding that although the only moment is NOW, that moment contains limitless manifestations.

Excerpt, "The Limitless Expression of Time," *A Time Traveler's Code* **of Conduct by Ruth #7**

TWO: *Journal Entry — October 19 ATL*

Agnes was adamant, "Regardless of what else might be happening, we have new assignments from the ATL Mission Office and a scheduled curriculum to cover!" As she spoke, she continued to wave her stylus directly at Emanuel #41.

"But, madame," Emanuel protested, attempting to explain his perspective again, "perhaps it might be advantageous in the matter of our ongoing education to discuss this issue of an alternate to the approved timeline, the possible ramifications of its creation, and just what might be done about it?"

Agnes stopped moving before us, eyeing our Swede classmate closely as she responded, "It might be advantageous," she conceded, although her words appeared to lack any conviction whatsoever, "but as this is now a matter of Core business and we report to the Core, our involvement seems entirely unnecessary!"

I added my own support for such a timely classroom discussion by inquiring, "And to whom does the Core report?"

Our instructress appeared angry, "Don't be impertinent! Until such time as the ATL Mission Office, members of the Core, or the Governor-General herself asks for our assistance, we will continue to focus on the scheduled curriculum."

At the sound of her own words, Agnes nodded approvingly and turned to face the whiteboard behind her. She appeared to collect her thoughts before stating aloud a name with which I was totally unfamiliar, "Pandita Ramabai." As she spoke, she wrote the name on the board, underlining it twice for additional emphasis. "Today, we will examine another real-world example. 'Pandita' is a title given to a Hindu scholar educated in Sanskrit, Hindu scripture, and philosophy, but let us refer to this learned woman simply as 'Ramabai.' She took occasion to point her stylus at the entire class, reminding us yet again, "This case history will be on the required final exam." She then pointed toward Manuela #64, advising her, "Pay close attention as this mission assignment is yours."

Manuela nodded, "Yes, Señorita, Agnes."

Our teacher continued, "I specifically want to examine timelines XVII, LIII, and CCXI." She wrote each of the Roman numerals before us, "These timelines possess the greatest challenge to the ATL, and will need to be addressed individually." She turned back to the class and added, "Perhaps it would be best to start with some background information?"

Although I could not help but smile, I refrained from looking in my roomie's direction, as I knew George would simply mouth back the very same words to me.

"According to the approved timeline, Ramabai was born in the middle of the Collective Illusion of the 19th century and lived until 1922. She was a strong proponent of women's education, social reform, and a champion for the banning of all child marriages." Agnes shook her head in dismay, "Do you know, that when she was born it was not uncommon for girls to be given by their own families for marriage when they were only twelve or thirteen and sometimes as young as nine and ten? Imagine!"

"Her family was part of the Brahmin caste, which is the highest social class in India. Her father was a scholar and often traveled throughout the country to give lectures on Sanskrit and Hinduism. He was very much ahead of his time as he believed in the education of women. He taught Ramabai how to read Sanskrit and encouraged her to study the vast Hindu texts, enabling her to become a scholar in her own right. Perhaps due to her father's influence and his own skill with public speaking, she would become an international speaker on all manner of women's rights and reforms, traveling throughout India, Britain, the United States, Australia, and Japan. Unfortunately, both her parents died during India's Great Famine and Ramabai was orphaned as a teenager."

Agnes returned to the whiteboard and proceeded to describe what followed, "At the age of 22, she married Medhvi." Our instructress dutifully wrote his name on the board. "This became a challenge for her from numerous perspectives. The first was that Medhvi was not a Brahmin; instead, he was a member of a caste below Ramabai's own social standing. It may be hard to believe but such a marriage was considered entirely inappropriate. He would also die two years after their marriage, leaving her a widow at the age of 24 with a one-year-old daughter."

She shook her head in dismay, "Unfortunately, one of the lowest tiers in Indian society was that of a widow without a family to support her. She was able to escape the hardship that confronted most women in her situation by supporting herself through public speaking and presentations where she recited Sanskrit, demonstrating her understanding of the Hindu scriptures. Her expertise was so proficient that scholars at the University of Calcutta conferred the title 'Pandita' upon her."

"She tried to enroll in Medical College in both India and Britain, but because she was a woman, she was denied admission. Eventually, she and her daughter traveled to England, where Ramabai enrolled in a teaching program. Three years later, she traveled to the United States, where she quickly identified with the difficulties of both African Americans and the Native Indians. Eventually, she published a book in English titled, *The High-Caste Hindu Woman*, which portrayed the plight of Hindu women, child brides, and young widows. Her work also led her to create a school for both orphans and child brides who had become widows."

Agnes paused and looked out at her charges before adding, "Brahmin custom prevented widows from remarrying. Widows were often considered cursed as they were seen as somehow responsible for the deaths of their husbands. They were required to shave their heads, wear substandard clothes, and exist on whatever food they might beg or scavenge. These same women were often subject to all manner of abuse! Ramabai's life made a real difference for so many who would have been considered outcasts!"

"Even though her life helped countless women, widows, and orphans, her name was purposefully left out of many books describing important reforms in the history of India." Agnes shook her head in disgust. "She became so frustrated with the caste system that Hinduism had placed upon those less fortunate that she converted to Christianity. Although her belief was that all individuals were equal regardless of their faith, she was condemned by many within her own country for becoming a Christian."

Our instructress tapped the end of her stylus with each of the four points that followed. "In spite of the fact that she has lost the prominence that should be hers in history, she began the Indian Women's Society, which promoted education and fought against the system of child marriage. She was a lifelong champion of women's civic and legal rights. She was an early proponent of India's right to self-govern rather than being subject to the British colonial system. And finally, for more than a hundred years after her death, the foundation she established would remain active, providing housing, education, and vocational guidance for widows, orphans, and the blind." At that point, Agnes slapped the top of her desk, "Those are the basics!"

"Now let us look at three timelines attempting to vie for prominence with the ATL. First, let us start with timeline XVII." Agnes pointed to the Roman numeral before us, "In timeline XVII, Ramabai is widowed at 24, but the all-male faculty refuses to confer the title Pandita upon her . . . Most within her male-dominated society believed that women were created to provide comfort and company to men; beyond that, they were relegated to focus only on procreation and child-rearing. Imagine!" Agnes appeared disgusted as she added, "Even within the approved timeline, the University of Calcutta did not grant any woman a doctorate until 1944!"

"Because Ramabai is never recognized in timeline XVII for her knowledge of Sanskrit and Hinduism, her life becomes subject to extreme poverty, and she fails to gain prominence as either a speaker or a reformer. She will die in her thirties from septic bronchitis and her daughter will be placed in an orphanage." Our instructress waved the stylus before us, "Obviously, this is a problem!"

Agnes turned back to the whiteboard and pointed toward the Roman numeral LIII, "The situation with timeline LIII is similar but even more horrendous for Ramabai. Once again, the University of Calcutta faculty ignores her education, and she ends up impoverished." Our teacher sighed, "However, in this timeline—as was often the fate of young widows in India—Ramabai is raped and dies shortly thereafter due to complications from the attack. Within the same timeline, her daughter is raised in an orphanage." Our teacher pointed the stylus at Manuela and affirmed, "This absolutely cannot be the outcome for this woman's life!"

She pointed the stylus at the Roman numeral CCXI, "In timeline CCXI, Ramabai does, in fact, receive the title of 'Pandita'—scholar—from the University of Calcutta, and for a while, her life proceeds in parallel to the approved timeline. However, once her abhorrence of the caste system leads to her own acceptance of Christianity, her work is repeatedly targeted by Hindu radicals. She is followed everywhere by those who would challenge and mock her. The end result is that both her work and her name became even more marginalized and unknown than they are within the ATL."

Agnes #23 stopped, appearing to ponder whether she had sufficiently covered the subject. After a moment of self-reflection, she turned toward Manuela #64, inquiring of our Latin classmate, "Are you ready for this assignment?"

"I am," Manuela said simply as she stood and walked toward the front of the class.

Manuela removed the Horologium mechanism from her pocket and began the five-step process with which we had all gained much familiarity: 1) She turned the hands of the watch counterclockwise, as she was traveling backward in time; 2) She closed her eyes and appeared to give thought to the mission before her; 3) Repeatedly, she stated aloud the name of her intended target "Ramabai"; 4) She moved a finger to press the "TEMPUS" button within the metal covering of her Horologium; and, 5) Manuela appeared to relax as she took a deep breath. In the next instant, she was gone, disappearing entirely from the classroom.

I should note that in spite of the numerous missions we had all previously undertaken, Agnes appeared just as nervous as she had been during our first assignment, anxiously bobbing about as Manuela proceeded with each of the five steps. Throughout the process, our teacher repeated the same litany of thoughts she spoke prior to every mission: "Things will work out just fine," "You are prepared for this assignment," and "You know what you are doing." However, I must confess that it proved difficult to ascertain whether her words, "You know what you are doing" were spoken in the affirmative or as a question.

As I have recorded on previous occasions, these time-travel excursions entail only the movement of one's consciousness to the intended location. It remains entirely unclear as to the whereabouts of the physical self during a mission assignment or even if such a self continues to exist for anyone engaged in the time-traveling profession.

When it was clear that Manuela #64 was gone, Agnes lifted several pieces of paper from her desk. She glanced momentarily at the information contained within each document regarding the remaining class assignments and then stated aloud the summary contents as she passed the pages to the intended recipient.

"Emanuel #41, destination Upper Egypt, 14th-century before current illusion, in the matter of Amenhotep IV, called Akhenaton, and the establishment of monotheism." She handed him the document.

Soeur Marie was next, "Bonne Soeur Marie #304, destination Iceland, 12th century present illusion, in the matter of Hrafn Sveinbjarnarson and his becoming the first Viking physician."

"George #111, destination Paris, France, 1895, in the matter of Alfred Nobel and the creation of his will."

Agnes glanced at the final set of pages, handed the document to me, and informed those present, "Ben #239, destination Han Dynasty, China, 2nd century before current illusion, in the matter of Zhang Qian's diplomacy and the creation of the Silk Road."

Once the ATL Mission Office papers had been distributed, Agnes reminded the class, "If you need additional information, go to the Akasha — Athena will be happy to help you. She knows everything!" She placed the cover upon her stylus, set it on top of the desk, and nodded approvingly before informing us, "Class dismissed!" She was quick to add one final reminder, "You need to be studying for that final exam!"

Not long thereafter, I sat with my three remaining classmates (George, Emanuel, and Bonne Soeur Marie) in the League Café. As there was no way to properly discern what period of time would transpire before Manuela's return, we decided to forego both the prescribed tedium of study as well as a trip to the Akasha for any additional information we might require for our new missions. Instead, we focused upon obtaining nourishment and enjoying the camaraderie among us. It was while I was taking a bite of my muffin and honey that George #111 chose to speak aloud a subject that had only been briefly discussed between us:

"Has anyone thought about applying for Athena's old job?" He quickly added his own thoughts on the matter, "It might be fascinating to work for Milton #71. After all, he is the League historian. One could learn a great deal in such a position."

Bonne Soeur Marie was the first to respond, "Pas du tout . . . not at all," she replied without hesitation. "It is the work of healing that I am drawn toward. I have no desire for an office job." She nodded to herself before taking a sip from her cup.

"It might be fascinating for a short while," Emanuel #41 responded, appearing to contemplate the idea for a moment, "but like Soeur Marie, I do not believe I would find fulfillment in such a vocation for long. Philosophy, theology, mysticism — these are the matters to which I find myself attracted."

After the three had provided their summary assessment, each turned to hear my own thoughts on the subject. As I had already considered the position,

I replied, "Although any purposeful employment may lead to contentment, I believe my own involvement with diplomacy shall provide the greatest satisfaction." My roomie-banker-friend appeared to contemplate my assessment before admitting, "For myself, working with philanthropy has given me a contentment I have found nowhere else."

"I cannot imagine who will end up in the job," Bonne Soeur Marie pondered aloud.

As I was facing the entrance doorway to the café and possessed the advantage of seeing Milton #71 coming toward our table, it seemed most fitting to verbalize, "We could always ask Milton." I pointed in his direction as he headed toward us.

Although slightly out of breath upon his arrival, Milton quickly volunteered, "I have just come from Athena and the Akasha Library."

Before he could speak further, Bonne Soeur Marie inquired, "Monsieur Milton, has anyone applied for Athena's former position?"

Milton waved his hand from side to side as if to suggest that the query was not of utmost importance but responded nonetheless, "We have sent a notice to all Wayfarers in the field and hope to find someone soon." He then repeated, "I have just come from Athena. Because of what she has discovered, I am recommending a background mission for both Ben and Bonne Soeur Marie. I need you to go to the library and discuss the matter with Athena. I want to inform the Governor-General of these latest developments."

He stopped speaking and looked first toward me and then Soeur Marie before describing the immediacy, "Athena is waiting for you! All other mission assignments or student activities are now secondary!"

I quickly took one last bite of my muffin, drank a

final sip of coffee that was no longer warm enough, and inquired of Emanuel and George, "Do you want to come to the library?"

The two agreed. Without further hesitation, we all left the League Café together, but as Milton proceeded down the long corridor heading toward the administrative offices, we four instead began the lengthy walk to the Akasha Library. It was a familiar journey, down one hallway and then another (and many more as well), before we finally entered the double doorway. I proceeded toward Athena. She stood next to a library table filled with more than a dozen volumes scattered before her.

She smiled briefly at me before hastily turning to the matter at hand. "I see Milton found you. I think I have discovered a problem."

I was quick to reply, "Milton #71 said you needed Bonne Soeur Marie and me to undertake a mission. Are you looking for information?"

"I am," came her response. She took several strands of hair between her fingertips, twirling them behind her ear as she contemplated what followed, "At least one of the timelines in opposition to the ATL is changing. Although it has always vied for prominence with the approved timeline, timeline CLII appears to be growing stronger. Because of our meeting with the Governor-General, I am concerned. The change is focused on Alexander the Great."

Emanuel inquired, "Has anyone within the League undertaken a mission to either that target or that period of the Collective Illusion?"

Athena shook her head and replied, "No. I believe this is somehow connected with whatever Emmett has been doing. Let me tell you what I know and what I have found."

She pointed toward one of the thick books on the table before her, "According to the ATL, there was a plot against Phillip II, Alexander's father. Many believe that Alexander's mother, Olympias, was involved. In any event, after the assassination of Phillip, Alexander became king at the age of 20. From the very beginning, he had military ambitions . . ."

As I watched Athena explain Alexander's history contained within the approved timeline, I must admit feeling some measure of pride that a woman such as this had chosen me to be her beloved. Truly, it was amazing to watch her chronicle events from the past with as much knowledge and understanding as one might discuss the curriculum explored by Agnes #23 earlier that same day. She provided a brief account of Alexander's childhood and upbringing, informing us that although there had long been rumors that he was a child of the gods, it was unclear from the records whether these reports had been widely circulated from his birth or had grown with Alexander's own repetition of them.

According to Athena, even as a child, Alexander was raised to believe that anything he wanted was within his grasp. His ambitions were encouraged. In addition to rearing him in all manner of military understanding, his father, Phillip, recognized that a great leader needed to understand much more than the art of fighting. For three years he was educated by Aristotle himself, one of the greatest minds in history. Alexander was intelligent. He was rational. He was restrained and self-controlled in most all things.

Athena was forthright, "On occasion his temper was extreme, and when not engaged in negotiations or some military conflict, it was said that he had a love for great quantities of wine."

As she continued her discussion, I was surprised

to learn that for 13 years Alexander had undertaken one military campaign after another and never lost one. Not once! Even when the forces he battled were far superior to his own, he had proved victorious. These military successes led to his being described by his contemporaries as "Alexander the Great," which further supported the claim of godhood — one who may have been fathered by Zeus himself. Athena ended her narrative by briefly describing his death:

"I have not had time to thoroughly explore the Akasha on every detail surrounding his death, and there is some variation given in accounts by his contemporaries, but it appears that Alexander became ill after a celebration. He was at the central palace in Babylon, preparing for another battle and eating and drinking to celebrate his own success. Some accounts suggest that he was challenged to drink a large bowl of wine himself, which he did, and shortly thereafter became ill. Others believe he was poisoned. Depending on the account, for the next twelve or perhaps fourteen days, he was weak, feverish, and had severe stomach pains. He appeared to be stricken with some form of paralysis and was eventually confined to his bed, unable to move. He finally died on June 11, in 323 BC, one month before turning 33."

"As it is unclear whether I need a diplomat or a healer to look into this situation, I am asking you both to go." Before finishing her account, Athena added, "I should probably let you know that after his death, the body remained in bed for at least six days before the Egyptian embalmers arrived. When they saw him, they were amazed to find that the king appeared very much the same in death as he had in life. His body had not decomposed in the least. There were no signs of blood, gas, or discoloration that always occurs after death. His skin was soft. Everything about him appeared normal.

All this led to further speculation that Alexander the Great was truly a god."

When she finished, it was my roomie George who asked, "What changes have you found within the opposing timeline?"

Athena replied, "Timeline CLII may be the shadow of the timeline we were watching earlier. I was able to find additional information that I was unable to verify within the ATL.

I was quick to inquire, "What does that mean?"

"Because the information is not in opposition to the ATL but instead simply supplements what we know, our system does not recognize a change. Since a problem has yet to be detected, there is no need for us to be notified."

George rephrased his query, "What is the additional information?"

Athena nodded and pointed to the books on the table before her, "The timeline does not indicate with certainty that Alexander the Great was dead on June 11. I need Ben and Bonne Soeur Marie to find out why."

Bonne Soeur Marie and I conferred with one another, quickly arriving at the very same conclusion. Our best course of action entailed a journey to the occasion when Alexander first felt some measure of illness prior to his death. We each took our Horologium in hand and proceeded with the five-point process. As we were both traveling back in time from the vantage point of the approved timeline, we began by moving the hands of our watch in a counterclockwise direction. I smiled at Athena before closing my eyes and proceeding with the remaining steps, ending with a deep breath and the sudden observation that I had started to fall.

As the falling commenced, I purposefully kept my eyes open as a means of ascertaining whether or not it would be possible to perceive Soeur Marie undergoing the selfsame process. It was quickly apparent that I saw only myself. This fact caused me to suppose, once again, that traveling through time entailed only the movement of personal consciousness.

In terms of my own perception, I possessed the awareness of falling, as if from a great height. I could feel the wind blowing against my body and its extremities, as though I swiftly descended toward the ground below. In spite of the fact that I had undergone this same manner of descent on every mission assignment, my heart pounded as if beating out of control. To be sure, both the classroom text and my own personal experience maintain that a Time Traveler has no influence over such a process. The sensation of falling continues until one's arrival at the intended destination.

When the falling had finally stopped, I became aware of being in the midst of some semblance of a large banquet. However, rather than being seated at chairs and tables, all those present (and I note herein that I could see only men among the celebrants) reclined upon long couches, relaxed on pillows, or found themselves prostrate upon cushions where they rested their heads upon one hand, held up by an arm and elbow, while proceeding to eat and drink with the other hand. I was surprised to find that most of the men wore flowers or leaves (or both) either within their hair or as a crown about their heads. My senses immediately became aware of the many aromas that filled the room: the presence of a perfume that was pungent with myrrh, cinnamon, and anise; the smells of food, basil, and onion; and the unmistakable scent of the twenty-some men who were present.

I knew that I resided within the consciousness of Alexander, as I could feel the thoughts of his mind and see the fingers of his hand reach for a solitary fig among the food-laden silver trays placed upon the small table before him. When he reached toward the platter, I could see the hazy outline of my own ghostly hand swirling in waves of motion, as if it was somehow connected to the form of Alexander himself. He took the fig inside his mouth, and immediately I sensed its sweet firmness within my own mind. It was then that I heard the voice of Bonne Soeur Marie.

"Monsieur Ben," she said simply.

Her transparent form stood but a few feet away and after giving some thought to separating myself from my intended target, I moved to stand beside her. No one within the room could perceive or sense the presence of the two vaporous forms standing before them.

The men had scattered themselves about the room, dining in repose or in some semblance of recline while young, male attendants scurried about to fulfill the requests of those they dutifully waited upon. They served fluted decanters of wine and carried ornate platters of gold and silver that had been filled with every manner of delicacy demanded by such an occasion. There were meat stuffs — including mutton, chicken, and rabbit — and small pastry-like morsels that contained fillings — I knew not of what. I could see beets, peas, mushrooms, and lettuce. And along with an abundance of figs, there were olives, apples, grapes, and pears.

The men conversed with the one or two individuals reclining nearest them or waved in acknowledgment to some comment that had been expressed by someone nearby. Although the language appeared to be some form of Greek dialect that I had never before encountered, I comprehended the thoughts and verbalizations of all those present. It was apparent that I stood in a company of men who possessed true affection and appreciation for one another. There was no thought of intrigue, conspiracy, or the planned assassination of a king. Instead, I was surrounded by the fellowship and camaraderie of jovial men who admired their brethren and had chosen to celebrate while consuming great quantities of food and wine. I observed aloud, "It would appear they eat well."

"I do not believe this is their usual fare," Bonne Soeur Marie replied with certainty.

I nodded and turned in the direction of Alexander, observing with surprise that even in recline it was apparent that the man was much shorter than myself. In spite of his stature, however, it was equally evident that he was a man of strength, exceedingly muscular, possessing a ruddy complexion, a strong forehead, and adorned with an abundance of hair best described as reddish-blond. I perceived a man in his thirties, very much in the prime of his health.

I stated the obvious, "He does not appear ill in the least."

Soeur Marie was quick to respond, "There must be a reason that the Horologium targeted this event."

We stood quietly watching the banquet and the celebration. It was not long thereafter that one of the young attendants brought a heaping platter of what appeared to be gizzards and onions and placed it on the table before the young king. Alexander smiled before greedily popping three or four of the meats into his mouth, chewing them ravenously.

As I stood and watched, Bonne Soeur Marie moved closer to observe the delicacy that had been set before him. She sniffed the plate two or three times before turning to me in alarm, "The chicken is nearly raw. This is where it begins."

Soeur Marie's assessment had prompted us to follow Alexander over the next several hours, as well as the days that followed. Although the young king appeared fine through the evening and for much of the next day, by the following nightfall he had become feverish, slightly tired, and chose to remain in the common chambers where he issued orders to his commanders for their upcoming maneuvers. When the meeting was complete, he returned to his bedchamber. He felt weakened and feverish, prompting him to call for the physician, Medius. However, the king's sickness was not severe enough to prevent the two from sharing a large meal and taking occasion to play dice and share a bowl of wine between them.

The four days that followed contained some semblance of normalcy but the sickness appeared to grow stronger. Alexander managed to undertake his normal rituals of bathing, worship and communicating with his senior officers, but his fever worsened and his ability to move about became hampered. A week after the banquet, he was unable to move, and his voice altered between extreme hoarseness and that of a mere whisper.

"He is nearly paralyzed," Soeur Marie informed me.

His paralysis prompted his generals and those

attending to him to surmise that their leader could be dying. As he had not made his normal rounds in several days, rumors began to spread throughout his armed forces that Alexander was already dead. The rumors prompted soldiers to encircle the palace, shouting and threatening to riot if they were unable to see their king. It was for that reason that Perdiccas, his most senior general, finally issued a command that every soldier within the army could pass by Alexander and express appreciation for his leadership.

Once plans for such a procession had been communicated throughout the encampment, the line of soldiers awaiting admission grew ever larger. In the end, it would take nigh unto a day to enable entry to everyone who desired to move through his bedchamber. Although Alexander could no longer raise his head unaided, or move his hands or arms in response, many claimed that they could see the movement of his eyes acknowledging their presence as they ushered past to speak with him.

While the procession took place, several of his officers journeyed to the closest temple, seeking an omen or a sign that the king would survive. Most of his generals, however, remained constantly by his side, only leaving the room when absolutely necessary. When every soldier who so desired had been given the opportunity to make a statement, and while Alexander still had presence enough to voice an occasional whisper, Perdiccas leaned toward his king, asking for counsel as to whom the generals should support as next in line. Alexander struggled to whisper only, "To the strongest."

The king made no additional movement nor did he voice any further command. It was late in the afternoon on June 11, when the physician Medius was summoned again. He looked upon Alexander for a few moments, speaking to him softly. There came no response. Finally, Medius took a small, empty serving tray from the tabletop and brought it toward the king's mouth and lips to ascertain whether the man's breath made any sign of moisture against the smooth surface. It did not.

As Medius conferred with the generals, I turned to Bonne Soeur Marie #304 and inquired, "He is dead?"

Soeur Marie moved forward and examined Alexander for herself. A look of surprise came upon her face. She moved ever closer, allowing her vaporous form to envelop his body. I waited, and I waited some more. I began to wonder why she had yet to respond and was near unto asking my question for a second time when I heard Perdiccas exclaim, "We must send for the embalmers!"

Suddenly, my classmate returned to my side and looked upon me with horror in her eyes, "The king is not dead! His breath is soft and shallow, and his heart is weak, but he is not dead."

"What do you mean?" I asked in astonishment.

"He has been paralyzed with Guillain-Barré syndrome. It is the process of embalming that will kill him."

When we returned to the confines of the Akasha Library, only Athena stood waiting for us near the table in the center of the chamber. Although she appeared tired, I was unable to discern how long she had remained in place, anticipating our return. Before we managed to speak, however, Athena informed us, "I found something."

"So did we," I said, motioning for Bonne Soeur Marie to

describe what had transpired during our journey.

Soeur Marie provided a thorough description of the entire background mission, beginning with the events of the banquet, and ending with the supposed death of a paralyzed king. Through it all, Athena listened with great interest, nodding in agreement at several points along the way.

When my classmate had finished her discussion, Athena explained, "It is unclear how much of this information was here before you left, or only found its way to the Akasha after someone influenced the timeline, but let me show you what I discovered in the 'things that are' section of the Akasha."

She lifted one of the volumes from the table and began to read, "Dr. Katherine Hall, a lecturer at New Zealand's Dunedin School of Medicine has proposed that Alexander the Great had Guillain-Barré syndrome, an acute autoimmune condition that results in paralysis. If this is the case, rather than death, Alexander would have been in a comatose state at the time of his recorded passing. As a large number of Guillain-Barré patients eventually recover fully from the condition, it would appear that Alexander the Great died not from poisoning, as had long been surmised, but from the process of embalming that was undertaken while he was in a coma. He was not yet 33."

As my sweetheart looked up from the text, I inquired aloud, "How might one catch Guillain-Barré?"

Athena replied, "It is the result of a bacterial infection," and then added, "the records indicate that a common cause is undercooked contaminated poultry."

Obviously, many factors contribute their own level of influence to each potential timeline vying for prominence within the ATL. Not only is there the power of persuasion possessed by any Wayfarer attempting to rectify the situation but the component of free will asserted by the target and all those directly involved retains a tremendous impact. In addition, the fact that certain outcomes in various timelines appear more prominent than others has caused a number within the League to believe that time itself may have some measure of influence over the Collective Illusion.

Your capacity to keep each of these components of influence in mind while maintaining an awareness of that which will be best for the Whole is the Prime Directive. For each mission assignment, a Time Traveler must hold to this central objective, as it is the only goal that may move the illusion of space-time and our own work ever forward.

Excerpt, "The Prime Directive," *A Time Traveler's Code of Conduct* **by Ruth #7**

THREE: *Journal Entry* — *October 25 ATL*

It was not long after the Alexander excursion that Manuela #64 returned from her own mission dealing with the potential timelines for Pandita Ramabai. As Agnes was extremely fond of classroom participation requiring us to present how various problems on our respective assignments had been addressed, on the afternoon following her return, Manuela stood before her classmates and gave a thorough description of each of the issues she had encountered on the various timelines.

Throughout the discussion, our instructress sat toward the back of the room making various notations within her ledger.

When she had finished, Manuela ended with a summation, "I am honored that I had the ability to work with and influence Señora Ramabai. Truly, she was a woman ahead of her time. She was brilliant, formidable, and a champion of those who were less fortunate. She made a difference in the lives of many women. Most certainly, the biggest challenge I encountered was in timeline XVII when the University of Calcutta professors refused to give her the title 'Pandita.' After several unsuccessful attempts to change the outcome, it occurred to me that each of these men had been raised by a woman," Manuela's words prompted her to smile broadly. "For that reason, I revisited the past and discovered that the mothers of two of the professors had been the very encouragement behind their pursuit of education and scholarship. I focused my influence on these two, eventually causing them to voice approval for Ramabai and the timeline became rectified."

She finished simply with, "The end."

Her words prompted applause from the class and Agnes nodded with approval as she stood to return to the front of the room.

"Thank you, Manuela," Agnes exclaimed just as she lifted the stylus from her desk. Once in hand, she waved it before us, "How about the rest of your assignments?" She peered at us with a look of frustration and awaited a response. When there was none, she added, "Ben ... what about China? Emanuel, Egypt? George, what happened to Paris? Bonne Soeur Marie, Iceland?"

"Mademoiselle, we had to deal with Alexander," Soeur Marie replied finally.

Agnes was quick to react, "Really? I understood

that only two of you were involved in that excursion and even then it was a brief background mission." The stylus continued to wave before us, while her excessive makeup caused her irritation to appear even more severe, "I need all of your assignments completed! Understood?"

We looked momentarily between us before Emanuel finally spoke, "Understood."

Agnes seemed to be considering further comments on the topic when Nashwa, her Middle Eastern friend, presented herself in the classroom doorway. "You told me to come as soon as I arrived." Nashwa waved a hand toward the rest of us, "Hello class."

Although momentarily startled by the interruption, Agnes was quick to regain her composure. She looked at Nashwa and smiled broadly. Suddenly, Agnes turned in our direction and verbalized only, "Class dismissed!"

As we departed the classroom, George #111 looked toward me, "Perhaps we should visit the library and obtain whatever is necessary for these mission excursions?"

I wholeheartedly agreed.

Not long thereafter, George and I found ourselves in the Akasha Library sharing a table between us. We had vowed to gather information dealing with our impending assignments, prompting several volumes from the massive collection to lay scattered about. I was in the midst of gathering insights regarding China's Han Dynasty and the diplomat and government

representative Zhang Qian, as I was completely
unfamiliar with either subject.

Suddenly, my roomie looked up from his text, "These
mission overviews are not nearly as organized as they
were when Athena pulled them together." George lifted
the summary document Agnes had provided and shook
his head in dismay, "This is missing some of the most
important information about my target."

I glanced toward him and inquired, "Such as?"

"Alfred Nobel left most of his estate to establish what
became the Nobel prize. An inventor and chemist, at the
time of his death he was extremely wealthy. His will
established a trust to honor achievements in chemistry,
medicine, literature, physics, and peace."

"Sounds extremely worthwhile."

My roomie nodded before continuing, "To be sure,
and all of this is covered by the document from the
ATL Mission Office. What is not covered is the fact . . ."
George reached for one book on the table while pointing
to another, "that Nobel made the greatest portion of his
fortune from the invention of dynamite—an explosive.
Although he invented dynamite primarily for mining
and as a means of clearing land for both roads and
construction projects, it soon became a central component
of warfare."

My eyes opened wide in alarm.

"The document also left out his brother's death and
the obituary that followed, which may have been at the
very heart of the trust's creation."

I was intrigued, "In what way?"

George pointed to the second book before him,
"According to the Akasha, when Nobel's older brother
died, the newspaper confused the man with Nobel
himself. Here is a newspaper headline from the time:
'The Merchant of Death is Dead.' It goes on to say

that Nobel became rich by finding ways to kill people faster than ever before." My roomie looked up from the volume, "This article may have prompted Nobel to want to do something to change his flawed reputation."

"None of that is in the summary document?"

"No," George replied, "Milton better find an assistant soon."

I heard Athena's voice respond from behind me, "He is interviewing a possible replacement at this very moment."

I turned about and felt a rush of joy as I gazed upon her. I quickly stood and embraced my beloved just as I requested additional comment, "Who is he interviewing? Is it, Emanuel?" I could not help but consider the possibility that our Swede friend had decided to pursue the position after all.

"Not Emanuel," she replied, "Her name is Louise #217. She looks about the same age as Milton. She was born in Normandy a long time ago and has been working in the field ever since her recruitment. Milton had me speak with her as part of the interview." Athena twirled a strand of hair with a fingertip as she added, "Louise told me she is tired of fieldwork and wants to settle down."

"Interesting," came my only reply.

George looked up and added, "It would seem we are getting our fair share of visitors today. Nashwa #86 arrived earlier, as well."

Athena nodded her head and affirmed, "Nashwa is meeting with the Core."

I was intrigued, "For what purpose?"

Athena smiled, "Even if I knew, I couldn't tell you."

"I have got to finish this assignment," I said before kissing her briefly on the side of the mouth.

"Are you finally looking into China?" she inquired.

I nodded again and retook my seat at the table with George.

"Okay," she said, "I've got my own work to do but if either of you need help, just let me know."

"Thanks, Athena," George was quick to reply.

"I will see you when you return, Ben," she said softly.

I could not help but smile.

Not long after we had shared a quick repast in the café, my roomie took his Horologium in hand and traveled to 1895 Paris in order to attend to the creation of a will for one Alfred Nobel. A moment after his disappearance, I departed for my own mission assignment to the Han Dynasty and this matter of Zhang Qian. I found my excursion to be as straightforward as these timeline conundrums can be and have therefore chosen to only record the issues of import. I should add that my own classroom presentation on the subject was filled with much greater detail, a litany of dates and names, and the extensive use of Agnes's stylus as a means of underlining both, thereby achieving sufficient credit for the assignment. For my own journal, however, herein are the primary issues of note:

As far as the approved timeline was concerned, Zhang Qian was a hero, a diplomat, a skilled negotiator, an emissary of trade, and greatly responsible for expanding the influence of China beyond the borders of its day. His influence opened the country to much of Asia, Persia, and the West. One of his early journeys lay the very beginnings of the Silk Road, which would eventually span more than 6,000 kilometers and prompt extensive trade and cultural exchange between East and West for more than 1,000 years. He would spend 25 years of his life undertaking one dangerous mission after another. Throughout that time, he would bring back to his emperor a wealth of information, goods, and promises of alliance. His own maps and detailed accounts of his journeys would stimulate treaties, trade, and even future military conquests. Centuries after his death he would become a Chinese national hero and was revered for his role in opening his country to the world.

Nevertheless, the central purpose of my mission was to address an issue Zhang Qian had faced on virtually every timeline. To be sure, it had become a major problem on more than a few. The crux of the matter was that during a trip in which he had been dispatched to meet and form an alliance with the nomadic tribes of central China, he was captured by a confederation of archers from the north. Ironically, it was this very confederation that his emperor had wished to form an alliance against. Once captured, Zhang Qian and those who had accompanied him were enslaved. This very matter had prompted my mission from the start as the enslavement would lead to a decade of hard labor on multiple timelines and to his death on several more. Even the ATL had him imprisoned for more than 13 years—a capture bringing disgrace to his name as well as the emperor who had sent him.

I must admit wasting some measure of effort from the very first on repeated attempts to prevent his capture and imprisonment altogether. Each of these attempts proved to be without success. Regardless of my approach or the chosen target of influence (on multiple occasions even targeting members of the confederation leadership), Zhang Qian never avoided capture. The northern confederation and the countless archers who supported their efforts were everywhere. Only when this recognition had finally entered my awareness did a different tactic come to mind. Being ever mindful that energy and persistence may accomplish even the most challenging of assignments, I decided to pursue an altogether different approach.

Although the northern confederation was immense, losses due to ongoing battles had created a situation of imbalance in which many women lacked the opportunity to secure husbands for themselves. It became a simple matter really, influencing those who enslaved Zhang Qian to direct his labors more in line with farming, counsel, and the pursuit of necessary chores among the populace. These activities put him in close proximity to females among the confederation and it was not long before several began to vie for his affections. Once he was married to a woman from the north, his level of oversight by his captors became vastly diminished. In time, he and his wife, and a son that had been born between them, escaped and returned to the emperor. Timeline mission accomplished.

Rather than being offered the opportunity to rest and reflect upon my latest assignment, however, no sooner had I returned to the League facility when Athena informed me that Milton had summoned me to the ATL Mission Office. With that in mind, I left my beloved in the library and made the long journey toward the administrative offices. After traversing through several corridors and long hallways, I arrived at the administrative wing, making note of the various office doorways that I passed: "Personnel," "Recruitment," "Student Services," "Recordkeeping," "Meeting Room 1," "Meeting Room 2," and then "ATL Mission Office," with the office of the Governor-General next door.

As I turned into the ATL Mission Office, I was immediately shocked to find the most striking blonde woman staring up at me from Athena's old desk. Her appearance caused me to catch my breath. To call her attractive was an understatement. I was immediately taken by her sparkling blue eyes, the silkiness of her blonde hair, and the glistening appearance of the skin upon her face. The marvelous scent of French perfume filled the air. She was beautiful!

She rose from her seat, "Bonjour, my name is Louise #217."

I gave voice to a stammer before responding, "Louise?" To be certain, this did not appear to be the woman Athena had recently described to me. "My name is Ben #239 . . . Milton wanted to see me."

She smiled, "Hello, Ben #239. Milton just hired me."

Before I had managed to collect my thoughts, the words, "I thought you were older?" fell from my lips.

She walked around her desk, took me by the hand, and led me toward Milton's inner doorway. "Have you not yet learned? Wayfarers may manage their appearance and time." Her other hand reached up and briefly touched the side of my face, "Is it not so?" She smiled, and then turned and knocked on Milton's door, "Ben is here to see you."

When the door was opened, I moved as quickly as possible to take a seat across from him.

"Thank you, Louise," Milton nodded approvingly. "Would you please let the Governor-General know that Ben has arrived?"

"Yes, sir," came her response but before shutting the door she smiled back at me, "It is so very nice to meet you, Ben #239 . . . I hope we will speak with each other again very soon."

Once the door was closed, I found myself stammering aloud, "I thought she was older?"

Milton #71 appeared totally oblivious to my discomfort, "She told me she was looking for a new start. She has simply chosen to let her appearance do likewise." I uttered only two words, "I see."

As I attempted to brush aside thoughts of the perils associated with my proximity to a woman such as this (momentarily even considering the possibility of bringing Athena on any future visits to the ATL Mission Office), Sara #11 was ushered into the office. I purposefully chose not to look toward the doorway as it reopened, turning my gaze to the Governor-General only when she had taken the chair beside me.

It was Sara who spoke first, "Ben, we need your help." She continued, "As you probably know, there was a meeting of the Core to discuss this issue of an alternate timeline. We are concerned. Assuming that an alternative to the ATL can be created, both Milton and Ruth believe that Emmett will use whatever influence he can in order to continue Alexander's reign far beyond the time set down within the ATL."

Milton interjected, "Should that occur, history suggests that Alexander will seek to conquer all lands bordering the Mediterranean to the south and west and eventually India to the east."

Sara was alarmed, "Much of history will be changed in an instant . . . and such a change might be extremely difficult for the League to rectify. We know that you and Emmett were friends. For that reason, the entire Core thought you might be the one most capable of addressing this issue before it becomes a problem."

I was immediately surprised, "Even Emma?" I could not fathom receiving her support on any occasion.

Milton sighed, "It has yet to be formally announced, but Emma #119 has been demoted from her position on the Core. Nashwa #86 has agreed to take her place and assume Emma's former responsibilities. Nashwa will be evaluating recruit recommendations from henceforth."

I interrupted, "What will Emma do?"

"She has been offered a position as a Wayfarer in the field," the Governor-General responded. "She has yet to commit to the assignment."

Milton leaned forward and spoke with certainty, "It would appear that we need someone to rectify any timeline changes associated with Alexander as soon as they occur. Can we count on you?"

"Absolutely," I replied, looking first to Milton and then toward Sara, "but if Emmett has plans to change the past, he will see my presence as soon as I attempt to intervene."

It was the Governor-General who replied, "I have thought about that, and I have an idea. When the time is right, we will discuss it further."

My roomie had just finished explaining his timeline assignment involving Alfred Nobel, the creation of his will, and the establishment of the Nobel Foundation in Stockholm, Sweden, the city of Nobel's birth. George stood before the class and Agnes #23 (who dutifully sat at one of the desks focusing upon her notes) and concluded by informing us, "As you have heard, several timelines had thrown the estate into question and more than one relative was eager to get control over Nobel's money. My mission was really to address the creation of the Nobel Foundation so that it could follow through on the terms of the will. Although he had no direct heirs, Nobel's relatives had fought the will, hoping to divide the estate between them. Due to the dissent of his extended family and the need to create a foundation to award the annual prizes, it would be five years between his death in 1896 and the first distribution of a Nobel prize in 1901. I am pleased to confirm that the timeline mission was accomplished."

He concluded with a simple, "Thank you."

We gave our customary applause and Agnes stood to move forward and take her place at the front of the class. Suddenly, a thought appeared to come to George's mind, as he took the stylus in hand and proceeded to write the number "31 Million" on the board behind him.

He spoke, "I should speak to you for just a moment about the time value of money."

Truly, it was apparent that my roomie would forever possess the mind of a banker.

George continued, "When Alfred Nobel died, he left behind $31 million Swedish Kronos, which was used to establish the Nobel Foundation. With that as the principal, the first Nobel prize in 1901 was around $17,000 U.S. dollars—truly a tidy sum even in the collective illusion of its day. With interest and investment gains, that original principal had grown to $6 billion Swedish Kronos 100 years later." He turned to write the number on the board, underlining it twice and adding, "It was then awarding prizes in excess of $1 million U.S. dollars. That will give you some idea of the time value of money."

For a moment, we classmates looked between one another as though pondering what we might do with such supplemental information, whereas George simply returned to his seat. Our teacher made her way to the front of the room.

"Thank you for a thoroughly enlightening discussion,"

she said as her head bobbed about approvingly, "I always appreciate having these additional facts."

She took stylus in hand, turned, and wrote the words, "Sevierville Time Slip" on the board before us. "Before we close for the day, I want to discuss the Sevierville time slip. Now let me say from the first that this is not an experience that most of those crippled by the Collective Illusion would ever encounter." She pointed the stylus at us and waved it dramatically about, "I am not telling you this story for that reason. Instead, I want to discuss this example because of a question it raises and that question will be a part of your final exam!" She peered out upon us with all manner of seriousness and added, "So listen closely."

"This experience happened in 1999, to a woman named Hattie Jennings when she was 68 years old. Because of the unusual nature of the tale, she only told the story to several friends as she did not want anyone to question her sanity." Agnes paused her narrative, shook her head in disgust, and queried the class, "Can you imagine someone criticizing an individual simply because they had experienced being out of time? What foolishness!"

Agnes turned and wrote the phrase "Family Reunion" on the board, underlined it twice, and then lifted several pieces of paper from her desk, "Let me share Hattie's own written account of her experience." Our instructress proceeded to read from the pages she held before her.

"'I have been married for fifty-nine years to a physicist (now retired), who I met in college. My husband's family is from the Great Smoky Mountains of Tennessee. In 1999 there was a family reunion, held on Memorial Day; with about 20 members of his family present. The location was a cemetery out in the country, near the town of Sevierville.'"

Agnes looked up from the page, "I want you to listen to how carefully she describes these details. She definitely has an amazing recall of the incident."

Our teacher resumed, "'We walked into the cemetery, where people placed flowers on some of the graves. Once that was done, we unloaded food and folding tables from the cars and trucks. There were a few folding chairs for the older people but since I was in my sixties and my husband was in his seventies we sat on a blanket on the ground. When the meal was finished everyone got down to the business of sharing information on family history. I had married into the family and had never met most of the people being discussed, so I had nothing to contribute. After a while, I realized that I was in need of a restroom . . .'"

She stopped reading to contribute her own thoughts, "I don't know how many of you have ever needed to use a restroom when there wasn't one available but obviously this is a problem. For that reason, Hattie snuck away, going further up the hill so she would not be seen. It was there that she attended to this business that needed attending to." Agnes glanced down at the pages and continued, "'After going to the bathroom, I felt much better, until to my absolute horror I found myself twenty or so yards from a house where a man and two children stood on the front porch. I couldn't imagine how I had missed seeing them. I expected the children to point at me and laugh but they didn't even look in my direction. It was a one-story house, unpainted, with a tin roof and a porch supported by four slender posts that ran across the entire front of the house.'"

Agnes interjected, "Now listen to how detailed she is when describing these people. 'The man appeared to be in his mid-thirties. He was thin, and his hair was a light reddish-brown, which is similar to my husband's mother's relatives. He was wearing a tan long-sleeved shirt and trousers. He had on brown high-top shoes. Both children had hair the same as the man, who I assumed to be the father. Both were barefoot. The girl was probably eleven years old. She was wearing an aqua blouse and a pink skirt. The boy looked to be about seven years old. He was wearing pale, gray cut-off pants and a green short-sleeved shirt. I watched them for a short while but as they made no notice of me, I decided to return to the family reunion back down by the cemetery.'"

Our teacher bobbed about with enthusiasm, and alerted each of us, "Now this is the exciting part. Listen to what happened next." Agnes continued, "'When I got back to the reunion, I asked if the people who lived up the road were relatives. Someone answered, 'Oh, nobody lives up the road. There used to be a house there, but it burned back in the forties.' I was so taken by surprise that I decided to walk back to where I had been. When I got there, there was no house, no family, and the area where I had just been was now overgrown with two-foot-high weeds. It was as if I had been in another time and place that was no longer present . . . I still wish that I had been able to meet those people and go into that house. I wonder if I could have done that and still returned to my present time? This experience was as real as anything that has ever happened to me. '"

When Agnes finished the account, she placed the pages upon her desk and informed us, "The question on your final exam is the same one that Hattie asked herself. If Hattie had gone into that house, would she have been able to return to the collective illusion of her own time? You will need to answer that question using any proof, documentation, or information that we have explored either in class or in the text. A simple 'yes' or 'no' is not going to be sufficient for this question!" She hit the top of her desk for emphasis, "I want backup confirming your answer. Is that understood?"

Although she was greeted with only silence, Agnes nodded with approval, placed the cover upon her stylus, and exclaimed, "Class dismissed!"

Ironically, the League has found that it is the misguided search for direction, purpose, or personal meaning that serves as the impetus whereby one may become lost and led astray. Once misdirected, those individuals may pursue power, wealth, control, or any manner of addiction to numb the sense that what they crave seems ever beyond reach. You must keep before you an understanding that ultimately the human creature is a seeker — seeking something extremely hard to describe beyond an awareness that it is lacking.

As a Time Traveler, you may believe your sole focus is the ongoing rectification of the ATL and amending timelines which vie for their own prominence. To be sure, this aim possesses immense value but it addresses the result of a problem rather than the cause. The cause is the loss of Wholeness, and at the core of humankind resides a deep understanding that the self was once complete. Ultimately, it is this very pursuit to become Whole once again that prompts all who seek.

Excerpt, "Perceiving the Self," *A Time Traveler's Code of Conduct* **by Ruth #7**

FOUR: Journal Entry — October 31 ATL

My roomie, George, and I finally found occasion to sit within the confines of our assigned chambers and cogitate upon some of the very issues with which we had recently been confronted. Although we rarely entertained guests within the room (as it was much too small and the League Café possessed the advantage of a constant source of refreshment), four chairs sat around our table. We peered at one another across the small tabletop, while George posed yet another query dealing with Emmett.

"Do you think Emmett has found some of the others?"

"You mean those who left the League?"

As my roomie nodded, I called to mind some of the names with which I had become familiar since my arrival at the school. "There was Melvin, Adda, Bruce, Gregory, Maude, and I believe a woman named Sybil . . ."

"That's right!"

"Truly, if I were Emmett, I would search out others who shared my frustrations. I should find it extremely boring to be alone in history. Certainly, a Wayfarer can influence individuals in history but without the ability to converse with anyone but self, the only certainty becomes one of monotony."

George #111 looked toward me as he pondered aloud, "How would you go about finding a fellow time-traveling rebel?"

I was quick to respond, "The easiest way would be to track their individual Horologiums but obviously that is only possible if someone makes a timeline change in opposition to the ATL. Without such a change, it becomes a much greater dilemma."

I considered the query for a few moments longer and then replied, "If I were alone and lonely, at some point I would revisit my own history in order to encounter those I had once known. By so doing, I might recapture the camaraderie of my past while negating the boredom of my present." My own words prompted me to nod in the affirmative, "I would wager Emmett is revisiting the original timelines of those who left the League."

My roomie agreed wholeheartedly, "That's brilliant!" He paused and then smiled with a twinkle in his eye, "Since I have your brilliance here with me, I have a query. How might you respond to Agnes's question?"

"What question?"

"Remember, the one about Hattie Jennings? If Hattie had gone into that house from the past, would she have been able to return to her own time?"

I leaned forward to share my thoughts, "Thus far, I have considered three possibilities."

He was quick to inquire, "And they are?"

I smiled and replied, "The three possibilities that come to mind are: Yes, No, and the prospect that such a question has no definitive response."

He motioned with his hand for me to continue, "I'm listening."

"Imagine the answer is, 'Yes, Hattie would return to her own timeline.' The proof seems to be indicated by the fact that in every real-world example and time slip story that Agnes has described thus far, never once have we heard a tale of someone bringing back something from that other time period to the timeline of their own experience. Remember the Hamburg time slip? Even the photographer was unable to retrieve a photo from the future. Perhaps it is not possible. If this is the case, even if Hattie did go into the house at some point her return to the very place she had started would be inevitable."

George chimed in, "And the rationale for No?"

"In response to, 'No, Hattie would be stuck in the past,' I offer the following. Our classroom discussions have made it quite clear that these time slip experiences are much more commonplace than we may have imagined. And if they are more common, it stands to reason that they have occurred throughout all of history. With this in mind, could they somehow be connected to the plight of individuals who have simply vanished from their own timelines? From my own time, I remember the story of David Thompson, founder of the New Hampshire colony. By all accounts, he simply disappeared one day in Boston. There was also Abigail Williams who suddenly disappeared from the Massachusetts colony right around the time of the Salem Witch trials . . ."

My roomie interrupted, "And George Bass, the British Mariner from my own!"

"I am unfamiliar with the name . . . Nonetheless, I believe such a listing of unexplained disappearances could be extensive. Although it is perhaps not the most usual outcome for these time slip experiences, we may need to consider that it is a possible one. If this is the case, we should consider the Hamburg time slip once again. We know that pictures were taken but the evidence vanished. Perhaps such evidence remains only when one becomes stuck in the new timeline?"

George appeared intrigued, "And the rationale that the query has no definitive response?"

I looked at him directly, "We must consider the possibility that Agnes is simply looking for a conclusive argument one way or another. If this is the case, any response will suffice as long as we provide sufficient evidence for our conjecture."

"That is definitely a possibility!" George replied.

Before any further conversation could proceed, there was a knock upon the outer door. I stood and moved toward the doorway, opened it, and was immediately delighted to see the face of my beloved standing before me.

"Athena!" I exclaimed joyfully. "Come in!" We embraced and I ushered her toward the table.

George stood to welcome her, motioning her toward a seat.

Athena appeared wide-eyed as she inquired of us both, "Have you heard what's going on with Emma #119?"

George was the first to respond, "What is she doing?"

"She is livid!" Athena grasped a strand of hair between her fingertips, twirling it as she spoke, "She is cleaning out her old office and is very upset about the demotion. She apparently shouted at both the Governor-General and Milton during their meeting and later demanded that Nashwa leave her office."

"She was spying on all the other members of the Core," I replied matter-of-factly. "It does seem somewhat unbecoming for an individual of her stature."

Athena interjected, "Emma doesn't see it that way. I heard her defense was that she was simply making certain everyone was doing their job."

George appeared perplexed, "But that wasn't her job!"

Suddenly, the three of us became startled, jumping from our seats as the blaring noise of the emergency buzzer began ringing throughout the facility. The alarm sounded with such intensity that any attempt at conversation — save yelling with all one's might — was nigh on impossible. George shook his head in frustration and pointed toward the doorway. Athena led the way with me and my roomie following close behind.

I turned to Athena and stated as loudly as I could without screaming, "George and I need to return to class!"

Athena nodded and replied with equal intensity, "I'll be in the library!"

As my sweetheart began her trek back to library chambers, George and I hurried in the direction of the school's classroom. When we arrived, Agnes #23 stood waiting impatiently at the front of the room. Manuela #64 was already present, and our remaining classmates entered shortly thereafter. While the noise continued, Agnes alternated between glancing at the pieces of paper she already held tightly within her hand and bobbing about with nervousness. One moment she was moving around her desk and in the next, she stared at the pages before her. At long last, the blasting sound of the alarm came to an end.

"Emergency assignment!" Agnes waved her stylus before us and then turned in my direction. "We have no choice but to move quickly, Ben! This one is for you. You won't have time to visit the Akasha. You will need to leave right away. We have a summary from the ATL Mission Office."

Our teacher turned to her pages for a moment longer before writing the following on the whiteboard, speaking the words as she inscribed them before us, "Mohandas Gandhi, January 1897, Mob Lynching." She underlined the sentence twice. "Your skills are needed immediately! The ATL Mission office is alerting us that timeline CDXVIII is vying for supremacy over the ATL. If that happens this man will be hung in South Africa . . . assassinated before his work is complete! That cannot occur!" She turned to point the stylus so quickly in my direction that I feared it might be thrown from her hand, "Are you ready?"

"Yes, Miss Agnes," I replied, journeying toward the front of the room. "What is he being hung for?"

Her appearance was somber as she uttered two words, "His race."

I withdrew the Horologium from my pocket and pushed the clasp. I turned the hands of its inner facing counterclockwise and closed my eyes to consider the timeline assignment. Although I could hear Agnes continually repeating, "You know what you are doing? You know what you are doing!" I pushed such thoughts from my mind and uttered the name I had only just heard, "Mohandas Gandhi . . . Mohandas Gandhi." With my eyes still closed, I pushed the TEMPUS button within the timepiece, breathed, and began to fall.

To be sure, as I made the timeline travel journey to 1897 South Africa, I collected my thoughts and pondered how best to assist this Gandhi fellow in averting the horrendous outcome portrayed within timeline CDXVIII. Prior to pushing the TEMPUS button, I had contemplated what might have transpired just prior to the attack, and it was that impetus that directed the moment of my arrival.

My sense of falling came to an abrupt end just as I found myself within my target walking the remaining distance down the plankway of a shipyard's dock to the boardwalk below. After encountering a brief moment of this man's confusion, I could sense the thoughts of Gandhi turning to his wife and three sons who had already arrived home. I perceived the vaporous form of my own legs in close proximity to those of my target as we stepped upon the boardwalk. Gandhi was a smartly dressed man of Indian descent, wearing the coat, tie, and trousers of an English gentleman and the tight-fitting turban of his Indian homeland. I suddenly became aware of the fact that he was a lawyer. A sign near the docked ship read in large, painted letters, "Durbin."

All at once, I heard the angry voice of a young man yell out from behind me, "Hey, Coolie, get off the damn boardwalk!"

As Gandhi turned his head to see who had spoken to him, I turned as well and gazed upon the outraged face of a white man standing with a group of a half-dozen others around him. None were as well-dressed as my target and not a one appeared as educated. The young man waved an angry finger at Gandhi and yelled again, "Move your gat off the boardwalk!"

Another man in the group added, "Flippin' Charro!"

I focused on removing myself from my target's bodily frame until my ghost-like appearance became separated. I stood next to Gandhi and contemplated the absurdity of these ruffians demanding a gentleman remove himself from any walkway simply due to the color of his skin. To be sure, even before my arrival at the League, I had come to the realization that equal liberty was the birthright of all. Obviously lacking that very awareness, the men continued to yell their insults, while a much larger crowd began to gather at the dock. A youngster selling newspapers (grasped tightly under one arm) stood nearby.

On the boardwalk traversing from the beach, I perceived a matronly woman with an enormous yellow parasol walking toward us. As she saw what was transpiring, glancing first at the gathering crowd and then toward Mohandas Gandhi, her eyes opened wide with concern.

"She knows him," I said to myself, suddenly becoming aware of the fact that she had just returned from her daily constitutional along the waterfront.

As Gandhi looked in her direction, the name "Sarah Alexander" came to his mind. In spite of her concern, she was too far distant and lacked any resource to render aid.

One of the men nearest the plankway pointed in Gandhi's direction and shouted, "Hey, that Coolie's Gandhi!" As most within the crowd appeared unfamiliar with the name, he added, "He wrote the bloody 'Green Pamphlet!'"

At the mention of such a tome, more voices began to speak out and half a dozen men scurried towards us. One of the largest men wearing dark suspenders and a wrinkled white shirt moved forward.

Gandhi immediately extended a hand as though to greet the man but his hand was swiftly pushed aside and the brute clenched a fist, which was delivered firmly against the side of Gandhi's jaw. My target fell to the ground as the crowd moved in closer. Another man picked up a rock and threw it just as Gandhi attempted to rise to his feet. An onslaught of rocks and sticks proceeded to cut the gentleman's face, arms, and suit.

"Let's hang the son of a bitch!"

Having seen enough, I took Horologium in hand and chose as my target one Sarah Alexander from earlier that selfsame day.

After what amounted to only a momentary leap as a means of arriving at my new destination, I was somewhat surprised to find myself within the confines of an office belonging to Durbin's Police Superintendent. My vaporous self seemingly floated within the body of Sarah Alexander as she spoke to the official sitting behind the desk before her. He appeared to be the officer in charge. Upon his desk were several copies of a printed green booklet emblazoned with the title, "The Grievances of the British Indians in South Africa." Sarah held the handle of her parasol with one hand and pointed to the booklet with the other, voicing her concern:

"It is unchristian what these people are being subjected to! They are British citizens."

The Green Pamphlet! I thought to myself.

The officer responded, "My darling, I agree, but it is hard enough keeping peace and calm without this damnable pamphlet. It is everywhere, and it is not going to help their cause. I wish Mr. Gandhi had never written it."

The woman was adamant, "Richard Charles Alexander . . ." she paused momentarily before beginning again, "R.C., Mr. Gandhi is a very learned man, a lawyer—a British citizen! He is simply trying to help. An indentured Indian is still a human being. Something has to be done to help these people and stop these abuses. They are looking for a better life."

The superintendent nodded, "Sarah, you know I agree with you, but no one wants their own ignorance thrown in their face. Too many men are already looking for a fight. We do not want to make it easy for them. We cannot."

Sarah sighed and then walked around the desk, leaning to kiss her husband on the cheek, "Okay, R.C.," she said finally, "I am going for my walk. We can talk more about this later."

The superintendent moaned softly, "I am sure we will."

A course of action suddenly came into my mind, and I made a quick jump to revisit the very scene I had encountered a few moments earlier.

Only a moment later, I found myself walking along the boardwalk within the frame of my target, Sarah Alexander. It was time for her morning constitutional along Durbin's boardwalk, only a stone's throw from the oceanfront. A gentle wind blew through the air, causing the ruffled embroidery of both her long dress and the enormous pink parasol to billow slightly in the breeze.

"Last time, the parasol was yellow," I said only to myself.

The scent of salt water filled the air, as I turned to focus on Sarah's own thoughts and repeatedly suggested that the day's forthcoming chores suggested a shorter walk was in order. I continually gave thought to the idea until, finally, Sarah spoke aloud, "I need to return home!"

Although she had traversed less than half her usual distance, she turned and headed back in the direction of the dock and the ship that had moored nearby. She was only a short distance from Mohandas Gandhi as he stepped from the plankway onto the boardwalk below. All at once, Sarah heard the voice of a younger man.

"Hey, Coolie, get off the damn boardwalk!"

As I turned to look at his outraged face, this time eight others appeared to be present. I mumbled to myself the words from Ruth's text, "'Once interaction with a timeline has occurred, space-time is altered ever so slightly . . .'"

Gandhi turned to look at the man, just as he pointed and yelled, "Move your gat off the boardwalk!"

Someone else shouted, "Flippin' Charro!"

Sarah quickly became cognizant of the situation and looked at those gathering to find a sympathetic face. When none became immediately apparent, she quickened her pace and journeyed in the direction of the young boy selling newspapers. She reached inside the tiny cloth purse tied within her dress, placed several coins within his palm, leaned down to his ear, and whispered so that only he could hear: "Run to the police station and tell them to hurry!"

As the boy departed with haste, the men continue to gather around the Indian gentleman, giving voice to one insult after another. Suddenly, one of those nearest the plankway yelled out, "Hey, that Coolie's Gandhi!" and then added, "He wrote the bloody 'Green Pamphlet!'"

A rumble of voices spread throughout the crowd as more gathered. One of the largest men, wearing a dirt-stained shirt and gray suspenders, clenched his fist and moved toward Mohandas Gandhi (who calmly extended a hand in greeting). The brute pushed it away and brought his fist against the side of the gentleman's jaw, knocking him to the ground. Several individuals threw rocks and sticks—some striking the man's arm and face, causing him to bleed. In the process, Gandhi's suit, shirt, and trousers were torn.

"Let's hang the son of a bitch!"

At that very moment, Sarah Alexander moved forward, towering over Mohandas Gandhi, just as he struggled to rise to his feet. She made a complete circle around him, swinging her parasol about in every direction. As she continued to encircle him, she spoke as menacing as possible, "Leave him alone!"

To be sure, it was the sight of such an image rather than the possibility of any threat that prompted many within the crowd to stop what they were doing. Some of the younger men appeared confused, others shouted to move the woman out of the way; a few began to chuckle at such a sight. Finally, the statement was yelled for a second time, "Let's hang the son of a bitch!"

Only then did I hear the sound of police whistles rise above even the angry voices of the crowd, and I turned to see R.C. Alexander and a dozen officers running toward us.

It seems appropriate to record within my journal what transpired after the arrival of Sarah's husband, the police superintendent. While the various officers dealt with the crowd, Sarah and R.C. and one of his remaining police officers ushered Gandhi away from the dock and to the home of a wealthy businessman and Indian immigrant, Jeevanji Rustomji. A doctor was called as several of Gandhi's wounds appeared serious. In very short order, he was given aid, and aside from his ruined suit, a sore jaw, and a few cuts, he would recover.

Mr. Rustomji looked upon the well-being of his guest just as Superintendent Alexander inquired, "Mr. Gandhi, do you wish to press charges?"

"I do not," came Gandhi's reply. "Most were young. They were confused and did not realize what they were doing . . . I would not choose to seek redress for a personal wrong in a court of law."

R.C. nodded.

While the doctor finished his examination, the sounds of a crowd gathering outside came through one of the windows. Sarah looked out and saw many of the men from the dockyard on the ground below, "They have followed us here!"

R.C. moved quickly. He turned to Mr. Rustomji and asked for a change of clothing. Once it was procured, the superintendent handed it to his remaining officer, "Put this on and give Mr. Gandhi your uniform."

When both the police officer and Mohandas Gandhi were wearing their respective change of attire, the superintendent journeyed outside to the front of the house and chose to speak with the crowd gathering upon the lawn. At the same time, the plain-clothed officer escorted a disguised Gandhi through the backdoor of the house.

In the end, the Akasha would record Sarah and R.C. Alexander as being ultimately responsible for saving the life of one Mohandas Gandhi. Without them, he would have been lynched in Durbin, South Africa in 1897, before ever returning to the country of his birth to lead the cause for Indian self-rule.

I should note that I came across this information within the library. It was also within the stacks of the Akasha that I made the discovery that this Gandhi would become known as one called "Mahatma" — a great soul.

George and I arrived at our classroom before any of the other students and even before the appearance of our instructress. It may be of interest to note that ever since Nashwa's appearance, Agnes no longer seemed as exacting in the timeliness of her arrival. As a result, my roomie and I were isolated within the classroom and our solitary condition enabled me to express more clearly my hesitancy in traveling toward the administrative offices unescorted.

My roomie shook his head in frustration, "Why do I have to come with you to Milton's office? Can't you go alone? You are only going to describe your suggestion for finding those who deserted. I do not understand my purpose in going with you."

My only course of action seemed one of complete confession, "Let me explain my concern thusly. In the past, I often found it difficult to withstand the temptation presented by any proximity to beautiful and flirtatious women. I must confess that Louise #217 is most definitely a beautiful and flirtatious woman. Therefore, I must conclude that Louise presents a temptation that I will find most difficult to withstand."

Although I had spoken the words quite clearly, for a time my roomie had neither inquiry nor retort. There came only silence. He looked at me and said nothing. When I could stand the quiet no longer, I finally demanded, "Have you anything to say?"

George smiled, apparently finding some measure of humor in the situation, "Yes, two responses come to mind."

I listened attentively.

"First, your statement presents a most excellent example of Aristotle's system of syllogism."

I frowned, and inquired, "And the second?"

My roomie's grin broadened, "Athena is going to kill you!"

Before I was able to comment further on the dilemma before me, the classroom began to fill. First came Emanuel, then Agnes, followed by Manuela and Bonne Soeur Marie entering close behind. Class resumed the moment Agnes removed the cap from her stylus, waved it enthusiastically before us, and provided an account of the morning's agenda:

"We still need to hear from Emanuel about his journey to Egypt," our teacher demanded, dutifully pointing the stylus in his direction, and then shaking the same hand toward Soeur Marie, "and Bonne Soeur Marie and her assignment in Iceland. These are the matters before us!"

Once Agnes had communicated her planned agenda for the morning, Bonne Soeur Marie #304 volunteered to go first.

For brevity, I choose to summarize her mission assignment thusly:

The Viking physician (whom for simplicity I have herein referred to as "Dr. Hrafn") was highly regarded among his people. According to Soeur Marie, he was quite skilled in a variety of medical treatments. In addition to the herbal remedies and midwifery of his day, he was capable of setting bones and cleaning wounds, and was extremely proficient at attending to injuries of warfare. Apparently, he had traveled much in his youth, gathering the best of contemporary wisdom from Norway, England, Italy, Spain, and France. He was also talented in the arts of iron and woodworking, and proved to be a capable poet and farmer. In addition to these talents and his skills as a healer, he was known for his kindness. His own farm often provided food and shelter for those who had none. Unfortunately, a longstanding property dispute with a neighbor would lead to his death on multiple timelines. My classmate described her mission assignment as follows:

"According to the ATL, Dr. Hrafn was supposed to be attacked and killed by his neighbor in the collective illusion of 1213. Unfortunately, several timelines had him killed ten years earlier than that. This was the mission I had to address."

"What?" my roomie appeared exasperated, "Why did he have to be killed at all?"

From where she sat, Agnes shook her head in frustration, "George #111, I do not understand why I have to keep explaining that ATL history is not haphazard! There is always a plan and that plan must be followed without exception!"

George sounded unconvinced, "What plan could possibly result from this?"

Agnes sighed, "I do not know every detail that resides within the Akasha for every tragedy or challenge in history, but I can assure you THERE IS A REASON! If you must find the answer, ask Athena when you are in the library. Athena knows everything!" With that, she added, "Bonne Soeur Marie, would you like to continue?"

My classmate then proceeded to describe how she

had influenced both Dr. Hrafn and his neighbor on multiple occasions, enabling his demise to be postponed until the very date specified by the approved timeline. On one occasion, she had even influenced the neighbor's susceptibility to an illness, prompting him to delay his assault. She described other instances in which she had influenced Dr. Hrafn to change his plans, thereby avoiding any confrontation with the neighbor that day. In the end, the learned doctor died as prescribed exactly as written within the ATL.

When she was finished, most of her classmates applauded in response. George did not. My roomie chose instead to shake his head in frustration. I should note herein that since the beginning of our recruitment there have been a number of occasions when even the rationale provided by the Akasha for a certain outcome in history's unfoldment has appeared less than satisfactory to him.

In terms of Emanuel and his excursion to Egypt, I wish I had been present for the entire discussion but I was not. I did learn that Akhenaton (who had originally been called Amenhotep IV) completely transformed the religion of Egypt, discussed the existence of one God rather than his predecessors' belief in hundreds, and moved the Egyptian capital from Thebes. His widespread changes were so foreign to his people and the Egyptian priesthood that after his death most evidence of his rule was all but destroyed and would not be known until 1887 with the rediscovery of Amarna, his capital—3,000 years after his death.

It was while Emanuel #41 was using Agnes's stylus to write "Amarna" on the board that a visitor presented herself in the classroom doorway. I looked up to see Louise #217 standing before us. The sight of her prompted me to gasp.

Louise looked toward our instructress sitting at one

of the desks and apologized, "I am so sorry, Ms. Agnes," she said with a French accent. "The Governor-General and Milton want to see Ben immediately."

Agnes was quick to respond, "You heard her, Ben! The Governor-General wants to see you NOW!"

Being somewhat surprised by the occurrence, it took me a moment to gather my thoughts. When I finally stood, I glanced briefly at George who whispered, "Don't forget Athena."

I sighed and followed the young woman out into the hallway. She smiled, took me by the arm, and led me in the direction of the administrative offices.

"Ben, it is so good to see you again!" I could feel her grip on my arm tightening as we walked.

"Nice to see you," I managed to reply, keeping my focus on the hallway before us and not the feel of her skin against my arm, the silkiness of her blonde hair, or the way her blue eyes seemed to sparkle in the light of the passageway.

As we walked along, her grasp on my arm suddenly turned instead to a gentle back-and-forth massage against my skin. As she touched me, she said, "I have been hoping you would come and see me."

I was able to clear my throat and respond, "I am seeing Athena."

The massage stopped and she squeezed my arm, "Oh, Ben, I don't mind. Maybe you can come to see me when Athena is busy?"

I quickened my pace, "I do not think that is a good idea."

"Well, Ben, the invitation is always open."

It was truly a relief when we arrived at the administrative offices. Louise smiled again and turned toward her office doorway. Before going inside, she blew me a kiss with one hand. I chose to move as quickly as possible into the Governor-General's office. I let out a sigh of relief as I took the seat next to Milton #71. Sara spoke first.

"Thanks for coming, Ben."

"Yes, thank you, Chap!" Milton added. "I think the time has come."

"What is happening?" I inquired, pushing the last thought of Louise from my mind.

Milton looked first toward the Governor-General before turning to me, "It appears that timeline CCLXXI is showing a very different outcome for Alexander's banquet. Although it has yet to exert prominence over the ATL, we need you to rectify the situation."

I nodded but mentioned the very concern I had expressed previously, "If Emmett is changing the past, he will see me as soon as I intervene."

Sara #11 leaned forward and stated unequivocally "Not if I give you this." She opened her hand and placed her own Horologium on the desk in front of me. "You remember what this can do?"

I nodded, "I remember. You used it with Emmett during the occasion of Ruth's recruitment. Pressing the TEMPUS button on your Horologium four times will render the user completely unseen by any other Wayfarer. Emmett will not even know that I am there."

It may be difficult to imagine any enticement that could prompt a Wayfarer to leave the work for which they have been recruited, pursuing instead the ability to bend time and history for a temporary, personal delusion. It is a choice that only a few have made. At best, it becomes a hallucination of space-time itself, without lasting meaning, purpose, or gain. At worst, it assists and prolongs the very illusion holding all of Creation ensnared by that which can never be.

You will come to the realization that consciousness will not be limited by those few who would use it for their own enrichment. It is neither a tool for power nor for gain. Ultimately, consciousness is destined for the Whole, for universal growth, and for that which is inevitable. Delaying this collective destiny amounts to little in the eternal but it remains tragic within the unfoldment of time.

Excerpt, "Choosing Darkness or Choosing Light," *A Time Traveler's Code of Conduct* **by Ruth #7**

FIVE: *Journal Entry — November 5 ATL*

I have rarely found occasion to be surprised at human nature but sometimes it does astonish me. Just such an instance occurred with Emmett shortly after my return to the palace in Babylon. Although my own device remained safely tucked within my pocket, I had utilized the Governor-General's Horologium so that my journey to revisit Alexander's banquet would remain completely unnoticed. As far as I knew, her mechanism was the only one that enabled its user to remain unseen even by another Time Traveler. After pressing the TEMPUS button four times, taking my customary breath, and undergoing the fall that is interwoven with these time-traveling excursions, I found myself within the target of one Alexander the Great.

As has been my experience with every target of influence, upon my arrival Alexander appeared momentarily confused but quickly regained his sequence of thought. I soon separated myself (and my waving transparency of a ghostly body) from the king and became an invisible witness to the banquet celebration before me. Immediately, I noticed that my vaporous self was surrounded by a thin silvery outline that moved in waves of motion with the rest of my ghostly form. This silver border was not something I had observed on any previous occasion, prompting me to conclude that it was connected to pressing the TEMPUS button a fourth time. Moreover, as I had not witnessed such an occurrence when Sara #11 had used the device in the selfsame manner it quickly became apparent that only the individual holding said Horologium could perceive its silvery outline.

I stood within the banquet chamber, gazing upon Alexander's soldiers who gathered before me. A few were still in the process of entering the room. I recognized Perdiccas, the king's most senior general, among them. Low-lying couches, pillows, and cushions had been positioned about the large chamber for the celebration. As the men entered they appeared to choose a place either according to rank, proximity to the king, or as a means of being near others with whom they wished to converse. To be sure, the timing of my arrival was perhaps 30 minutes earlier than when I had last made the journey with Bonne Soeur Marie. Although I had not focused on the specific attire of the various soldiers during my previous excursion, it did appear that a number of those present had adorned themselves with red sashes and colorful tunics as opposed to the mostly white apparel I remembered from before. ("Once interaction with a timeline has occurred, space-time is altered ever so slightly.")

Already, large decanters of water and wine had been placed near small bowls on short tables scattered throughout the room. The ornate platters of silver and gold were just being ushered forward by young male attendants. Most of the trays were brimming with an abundant supply of fruits and vegetables. There were also great quantities of bread, olives, and figs. I saw hand-sized pastry filled with morsels of cheese, more olives, and perhaps tiny tidbits of meat.

Muscular men reclined upon pillows or couches or lowered themselves to the ground, resting their heads (most frequently adorned with flowers or leaves) upon one hand, while the other hand reached toward some foodstuff or beverage that had been placed before them. I watched many of those present pour some portion of water in the bowls upon the small tables and then mix in a quantity of wine, achieving their desired taste in the process. Many appeared most fond of dipping bread into this wine mixture and then placing the moistened loaf into their mouths. It was while I gazed upon the proceedings of the banquet that Emmett, former keeper of the records, appeared before me with someone I knew not. Although Emmett's hair remained a brilliant white (matching the color of his attire), he appeared considerably younger than he had looked during our last encounter.

"Why are we here?" asked the vaporous form of the red-haired man standing next to him.

As Emmett was nearly a head taller, he glanced down at the shorter man and replied, "We are assuring

the outcome." His own ghostly image moved in waves
of motion as he turned about the room and appeared to
take account of the situation.

"I don't understand." The red-haired man seemed
frustrated, "We need to focus on the duplicate ATL. The
approach you have chosen means there is much more
that needs to be done."

Emmett's eyes opened wide as he spoke with
authority, "Bruce, as I have told you from the very first,
there are reasons for what we are doing. I would also
advise that you not underestimate Sara #11. Milton's
awareness of history may also prove to be a tremendous
challenge for us."

Bruce #29! I thought to myself. The League's head
teacher before Agnes had assumed the role.

"To be sure," Emmett added, "this is only a diversion.
But it is a diversion for them, not for us. While they focus
on resolving this situation, we will attend to our own
timeline." Although Emmett turned and looked in my
direction, I remained unseen, completely motionless,
and quiet. He said finally, "Hurry, they will be here
soon."

Bruce nodded and inquired, "What do you want me
to do?"

"I need to influence Alexander so that this outcome
becomes much more difficult to rectify," Emmett replied
and then pointed toward a door where an attendant
scurried forth with a platter of figs, grapes, and dates.
"The food is being prepared through that doorway.
One of the cooks has been laboring for hours and is
overwhelmed. The last time I was here, she undercooked
a dish for the king. I need you to make certain that she
cooks it thoroughly."

Bruce nodded and soon exited the room. Emmett

moved toward Alexander and then closed his eyes in the manner of a Wayfarer about to influence a target.

As I was uncertain as to whether Sara's Horologium made the sound of myself imperceptible to another Time Traveler, I crept as cautiously as possible toward Emmett and the king. As I moved, I caused my own breathing to become soft and shallow. With my movements, the silvery outline that contained me continued to hover about. When I was as near to Emmett as I thought safe, I closed my eyes and attempted to feel whatever ideas were entering into the mind of the king. After only a moment, I knew it had something to do with India being put forward as a target of conquest. It was there that Alexander was encouraged to lead his troops into battle.

A voice interrupted us, "I have taken care of it." Bruce #29 continued, "The gizzards and onions will be cooked thoroughly."

Emmett opened his eyes, nodded, and replied, "We need to go. They will be here shortly." A moment later the two vanished completely from sight.

I must confess that the idea of Emmett purposefully trying to distract us with a timeline decoy was not something that had previously entered my mind. It appeared that the changes upon timeline CCLXXI were nothing more than a distraction, but it was a distraction I believed I could bring to a quick end. As I contemplated the best way to address the situation before me, I saw the vaporous images of first Bonne Soeur Marie and then my other self appear within the room. I observed the other me become aware of the banquet and the celebrants who were present. I watched him make note of the flowers and leaves that adorned the soldier's hair, the novelty of reclining upon the ground to take one's meal, and the various foods and smells that were present.

"Monsieur Ben," Bonne Soeur Marie addressed my other self.

As both the banquet and the arrival of the two travelers appeared to be following the proper course of events, I proceeded to the kitchen beyond the banquet chamber. Upon entering, I made note of the contrast between the celebration of soldiers drinking wine, eating delicacies, and relaxing in conversation with those around them and the intense hubbub of the activity before me. The kitchen and most of those present were in an uproar. Attendants waited impatiently for scullery maids to refill fruit and vegetable platters, or spoke irritably to cooks about how the dish they waited upon was taking far too long to prepare. The noise of voices, clattering platters, and the chaos of all those present filled the room. The kitchen was far too warm (as the heat from the cooking fires was constant), adding to the irritation of those present. Someone dropped one of the silver trays, causing the tone of the exasperated to grow even louder.

In the midst of such commotion, I perceived the plate of gizzards and onions that had prompted Alexander's sickness to begin with and moved toward the cook who had prepared such fare. Sweat dripped from the woman's forehead. Her attire was covered with stains, a variety of foodstuffs, and speckles upon her apron with the appearance of blood. Nothing about her or her workstation appeared sanitary. Upon the table next to her was a large bowl of raw gizzards with a bowl of onions nearby, both waiting for their turn at the flames. In addition to the gizzard dish, she seemed responsible for a continuous supply of small pastries as she took quick turns pressing the dough before her, filling it with cheese and various morsels, and then placing the concoction for a few minutes in the brick oven beside her. From her own thoughts, it was clear that the woman felt her labors endless.

The plate of gizzards that Alexander had devoured during my previous visit had been moved apart from the flames but remained close enough to the heat to retain their warmth. I believed that the best course of action was to ruin the gizzards before me and cause the cook to begin again. With that in mind, I focused my Wayfarer's influence upon her, suggesting that the gizzards needed to be a little warmer before they could be served. The thought prompted her to move them back toward the flames. I then proceeded to fill her head with the need to focus on the pastries and the never-ending mouths to feed beyond the kitchen doorway. When such had entered her mind, she began to form together one small pastry after another in order to keep up with the demand. While in the process of such assembly, she forgot all about the gizzards. Before long, they were burned beyond recognition.

"By the dog!" the cook screamed in frustration as she perceived what had happened to her gizzards and onions. She quickly grabbed the pan and tossed what it contained aside. As swiftly as possible, she pulled together the ingredients (gizzards, onions, and seasonings) for the very same dish and moved them toward the flame. A moment later, one of the male attendants stood impatiently before her.

Using my influence, I prompted her to forget the length of time the dish had been within the flames and while the gizzards were still raw she scooped them into a serving dish and quickly passed them to the attendant before her, "For the king," she said with exhaustion.

I followed the attendant into the banquet room and waited while he placed the dish before Alexander. The king smiled and greedily popped three or four of the meats into his mouth, chewing them ravenously.

When it appeared that the timeline had been rectified, and knowing full well that George would be horrified by maintaining the ATL in such a manner, I took Sara's Horologium in hand and returned to the League.

Upon my return, I gave the Governor-General her Horologium and alerted both Sara #11 and Milton #71 to the fact that the changes upon the timeline had been rectified but that they were simply a diversion to some grander scheme Emmett held in mind for his duplicate ATL. I also discussed the presence of Bruce and my own suspicions that Emmett was collecting former Wayfarers as part of his plans. After my meeting within the Governor-General's office (and spending as little time as possible in the vicinity of Louise #217), I soon found myself within the classroom being subject to what Agnes chose to call a "review session." The words had been written (and underlined) upon the board.

Our instructress bobbed before the five of us and inquired, "What is most true about the nature of time?"

Manuela #64 raised a hand, and Agnes pointed the stylus in her direction.

"Señora," Manuela began, "what is most true about time is simply that there is only NOW."

Agnes nodded, and queried, "Who can tell me at least one reason why the League just doesn't go back and eradicate from the moment of their own recruitment someone like Emmett, or Bruce, or Sybil and be done with their foolishness once and for all?"

Emanuel #41 raised his hand but spoke instead of waiting to be called upon, "Madame, innumerable paradoxes would result by doing such."

The instructress waved her stylus toward him, "I need an example."

"Very well," our Swede classmate continued, "if we were to go back and eradicate Bruce, making it so he was never recruited in the first place, what would happen to all of the students he taught during his time as head instructor? Who would have taught them or would they even be educated at all? Would they still be Time Travelers? What would happen to all of the mission assignments he undertook as a Wayfarer? Would these timeline missions be reset back to their original problems? Would reset timelines vie for prominence with the ATL? What would happen to all of the knowledge and information Bruce's actions and efforts contributed to the Akasha? Eradicating him from recruitment would create a paradox of enormous complications."

"Exactly!" she slapped her hand on her desktop. "And it is for that reason the Core needs to capture these rebels and return them to one hour after their recruitment. In this manner, the ATL remains intact and they are left to face the normal process of their demise . . ." She paused as though to consider the next query of import and then asked, "Now who remembers the restraints that continue to empower the illusion of time?"

George and Emanuel immediately lifted a hand to be called upon but Agnes turned instead in my direction, "Are you participating with the rest of the class, Ben #239?"

"Certainly," I responded, "there is the clock, the calendar, and the creation of time zones."

"Good!" she replied, "now if the final exam asks

for additional details on any of these you will need to provide those additional details!" She looked around the classroom before inquiring, "Who wants to describe why the League only focuses upon historical episodes within timelines that are vying for prominence with the ATL?"

Emanuel raised a hand but rather than waiting to be called upon, he responded, "Madame, throughout the Collective Illusion there are perhaps limitless renditions of the very same event in history. Some of these events reside within lesser timelines; others reside upon timelines vying for prominence. Any historical happening upon a prominent timeline has the potential to displace that very incident upon the ATL."

"Correct!" came her enthusiastic response. "You could also say that as long as a timeline remains a lesser timeline, it cannot impact the ATL!" She waved the stylus at the entire classroom for emphasis. "Next," she continued, "who wants to describe the Prime Directive? George #111?"

George nodded, "I would describe it as a model of behavior in which a Wayfarer must keep foremost in mind an understanding that every action should be in keeping with what is best for all concerned on any mission assignment."

"I would accept that!" Agnes nodded approvingly. Suddenly, she squinted her eyes and peered about the room as if she was about to reveal the most amazing secret, "Let me tell you one of the questions on the final. There will be an essay in which I ask you to describe IN DETAIL . . . (the words were spoken much louder than the rest) any two of the following time slip accounts: the Medieval time slip, Asahi's April time slip, the Moberly-Jourdain time slip, Victor Goddard's time slip, the Hamburg bombing time slip, the Abbeville time slip, the Sevierville time slip . . ."

Bonne Soeur Marie interrupted, "I do not recall this Abbeville time slip?"

Agnes bobbed excitedly before us, "That's because we haven't discussed it yet, but it is an amazing story! It is on your schedule for next week." She paused for only a moment before continuing with her review, "Now, who wants to remind the class of any of the real-world examples we've discussed that prove beyond any doubt whatsoever that time is without meaning?"

As our instructress looked about the room for someone to respond to her query, my mind turned first to Emmett and then to Ruth and all she had told me about what might be done with a duplicate ATL.

It came as quite a surprise for our class to learn that Agnes #23's curriculum had been postponed as we were all being "recruited," which is how Milton #71 chose to describe the situation. Although I might have expected Agnes to become frustrated by the deferral of her planned coursework, instead she appeared totally mesmerized standing at the back of the classroom with the Governor-General next to her on one side and Nashwa #86 on her other. Emma #119 and her horned-rimmed spectacles had taken a seat by herself at the end of a row, staring angrily at anyone who looked in her direction. Ruth #7 and Elder Professor Grimwald were seated near the back. Athena was at a desk on my right, whereas George was seated on my left. I knew that Louise #217 had taken a seat somewhere behind me as I could smell the scent of French perfume wafting through the air. I chose not to look in her direction. Instead, I stared toward the front of the classroom as Milton explained the task which confronted us:

"The Core has repeatedly discussed this situation and what might be done about it. We have also relayed our thoughts and our suggestions for dealing with the problem to our members in the field. As you were informed previously, the creation of a duplicate ATL has the potential to create a crisis of immense proportions. Recently . . ." he gestured in my direction, "Ben #239 has informed us how Emmett might go about finding and gathering those who have left the League. We must do whatever we can to prevent this from happening. Although anyone who has deserted the League might become troublesome to our efforts, a group of them working together could pose a tremendous threat to our work and the entire stability of the ATL."

Milton lifted the stylus from Agnes's desk and wrote seven names on the board: "Emmett, Bruce, Adda, Melvin, Maude, Gregory, Sybil." Once the names were before us, he continued, "We know that Emmett has already tracked down Bruce. Assuming that Emmett has yet to find them all, we must do whatever we can to discover the whereabouts of Adda, Melvin, Maude, Gregory, and Sybil before he does . . ."

"They need to be returned to one hour after their recruitment and eradicated!" Agnes interrupted from the back of the room.

"That is the plan," Milton conceded.

It was our Swede classmate who inquired, "What are you proposing we do?"

Milton nodded, "To begin, we will need Athena to pull together a listing from the Akasha of the most notable life events for each of these individuals on their original timelines. Using the idea proposed by Ben, these are the periods in history where we will place our focus. We are going to separate into three teams. I will lead one, Sara will lead another, and Ruth will lead a third."

Milton stopped speaking and pointed behind me, "Yes, Louise?" Apparently, she had raised her hand.

"If you need me to be a part of a team, perhaps I could be of some assistance to Ben . . . or one of the others?"

Athena turned to me with some measure of confusion upon her face and then looked back in the direction of Louise. Milton responded: "I think it would be best if you remain in the ATL Mission Office. We also want Agnes and Nashwa to stay behind in case anything else of consequence comes to the attention of the League. That means we are going to have five students and four members of the Core taking part in this mission—a mission to find any of the rebels before Emmett can find them."

As the students looked between themselves, Milton wrote his own name on the board followed by Bonne Soeur Marie and Emanuel. After writing Sara's name, he wrote Manuela and Grimwald. Finally, the names Ruth, Ben, and George were scribbled before us. It was in just such a manner that three teams were created.

George turned to me and inquired, "Are you ready to find some Time Travelers?"

It was later that same afternoon that each of the teams gathered within the central chamber of the Akasha

Library. Athena had already pulled together three documents noting the most significant events within the lives of Adda, Sybil, and Gregory. After placing the materials before us (and smiling briefly in my direction), she departed down one of the library corridors to gather similar documentation for Maude and Melvin, who would be next on the list. There was a brief conversation between Milton and the other Core members where it was decided which team would pursue which rebel. In the end, Milton and his group took the information concerning Adda; Sara's team decided to search for Sybil; and Ruth, George, and I would be in pursuit of Gregory.

After the others had gone, George turned to Ruth #7 and inquired, "Can you tell us anything about Gregory?"

Her comely face turned toward him and she nodded, "Yes, I knew him."

I noted (not for the first time) that although she chose the appearance of a young woman, her eyes sparkled with the wisdom of one who was far, far older.

"I knew him well," she repeated and then added, "More than anything else, he was an idealist. He had such hopes when he arrived, but in time, the realities of our work seemed to take their toll. It became all too clear that he came to regret becoming a part of the League."

"What did he do prior to his recruitment?" I inquired.

"He was but a simple farmer. His dream was to be of service to those less fortunate than himself. For a time, he entered a seminary and thought the Church might be his path. Very quickly, however, he came to believe that the hierarchy, the rules, and the struggles for internal power were much more prominent than any desire to help those in need." She paused, looked between us, and added, "He returned to farming, married, and would eventually have seven children of his own. He was a kind man, always helping those he could within his small town. For the rest of his life, however, he never lost the dream of being of service to others. It was the intensity of that very desire which prompted his recruitment."

Ruth passed the document detailing the highlights of Gregory's life to my roomie, who scanned it for several minutes before passing it to me. What I read suggested that in addition to service, he possessed a deep love for his family. When I had finished glancing through the pages, George turned to me and inquired, "Where should we begin?"

As I pondered the query, it was Ruth who chose to respond, "Gregory #143 held a deep love for his wife and children. Perhaps we should begin with occasions when they were together?"

Obviously, within the life experience of most individuals resides an abundance of notable events, important encounters, and memorable moments. In addition to all manner of holidays and celebrations, there are frequent gatherings for the inevitable transitions in life, including births and deaths and weddings and departures. When one considers the life of a farmer, there is an additional measure of noteworthy experiences associated with planting and harvesting and the seasons, and all manner of activities tied to animal husbandry from the shearing of sheep to the birthing of calves. An immense variety of all these things quickly become apparent in the life of Gregory as I had stood witness to more than a dozen such occasions along his personal timeline. As I watched his life unfold before me, I could not help but be led to one unmistakable conclusion: I liked the man. I truly liked the man.

We three stood as vaporous spectators against one wall of the small cottage. Ruth stood between my roomie and me as we watched, yet again, the activities of Gregory and his family. On the other side of the room was a fireplace and hearth, the flame of which gave forth sufficient warmth for all those within. Just as we had witnessed on previous Christmastides, the season called for the fireplace to be decorated with green holly and bright red berries. Upon the table in the center of the room was a large basket surrounded by foodstuffs and a few carved figurines. One of the daughters tied a small bow of holly to the handle, while Gregory's wife, Miriam, made the finishing touches on her mince pie. An elder daughter stood nearby, holding the family's smallest child in her arms.

"Do you think they will be surprised?" the younger girl inquired.

"Perhaps," Miriam said with a smile.

"Do you want me to get the eggs yet, Mama?" the older girl asked as she comforted the infant.

The mother looked toward her husband and two sons in the corner of the room as if to ascertain the status of their labors before replying, "A little while longer. We want to put them in the basket after the toys so that the eggs do not break."

I have long contended that virtue alone is sufficient to make oneself great, glorious, and happy. From all I had witnessed, Gregory appeared to be just such a man. He had a kindly face and a gentle spirit. He sat within his corner chair skillfully carving the final features on a small wooden figure that appeared to be a knight.

Although he gave focus to the work before him, he repeatedly looked at each of his sons and nodded with approval.

"How can you make these so fast?" the older boy asked.

Gregory smiled, "Lots of practice." He reached out and patted the young man on the back, giving reassurance, "You are doing just great. You both are!"

The older boy continued carving his own figurine, while the youngest son sat upon the floor carving what appeared to be a spinning top.

"I want to be sure all the children have a toy," the youngest son asserted.

"That is wonderful, son," Gregory said proudly. "That is wonderful."

As I looked about the room, standing as witness yet again to the family's industriousness and their desire to be of aid to others, Ruth voiced her thoughts aloud, "Perhaps we have been mistaken. We will not find Gregory amidst these times of joy and contentment." She said with certainty, "He is not unresolved about occasions such as these."

I turned and inquired, "Where then?"

She looked directly into my eyes, "I would imagine he is near to the time of his greatest regret . . . the occasion of his own recruitment."

Shortly thereafter, we returned to the bedroom of the very same cottage. Years had passed, decades in fact. Miriam had become a frail, old woman and sat in a chair next to her husband's bedside. Moisture filled her eyes but her tears appeared spent. Gregory lay quietly on his bed. The only sound he made was an occasional moan as breath struggled to fill his lungs. Two grown men stood at the foot of the bed but it was difficult to ascertain if these were the very same boys I had seen in their youth or if these were Gregory's other sons. A middle-aged woman stood behind her mother's chair, patting the elder woman's shoulder from time to time.

"Can I get you anything, Mama?" the woman asked.

"It won't be long now," Miriam mused aloud.

On the other side of the bed across from Miriam's chair, the vaporous forms of Ruth, George, and I stood and watched, and waited. We served as quiet observers. Thus far, there was no sign of Gregory as Wayfarer.

After a considerable time, it was my roomie who stated, "Obviously, Gregory will see us."

Ruth nodded, "Yes, as will his recruiter."

My roomie's eyes opened wide with surprise, "What will we do?"

Ruth was undisturbed, "Leave that to me."

I was near to verbalizing an inquiry as to who had recruited Gregory in the first place when Hakim #60, the tallest ebony-colored man from the Core materialized before us. Obviously, I knew him from my time at the League, and well-remembered Professor Grimwald's description of him, "At six-foot-eight, you will find him the tallest among us." But seeing his form within the small chamber caused his appearance to become even grander.

Hakim looked first to bed, and the dying Gregory and then appeared to gasp as he looked upon the ghostly image of the three of us, "Ruth?" He managed to inquire. To be certain, at this point in the approved timeline, Hakim had yet to ever encounter either George or me.

"Hello, Hakim," Ruth replied gently. "Continue with your recruitment. We are here for a background mission."

Hakim turned first to me and then to my roomie, George. Before he could speak what was on his mind, Ruth was straightforward, "These are Wayfarers. You will meet them later along the ATL. They are friends of yours. Proceed with your recruitment so that we might undertake our own assignment."

Her words seemed to satisfy him, as he nodded and turned back to the bed and spoke aloud, "Gregory . . . Gregory, can you hear me?"

The man on the bed groaned, prompting Hakim to repeat himself, "Gregory, can you hear me?"

All at once, I began to witness something most unusual. Although the sleeping form of Gregory remained quite still (only giving forth an occasional groan as it struggled to take breath), a vaporous outline began to encircle the man's entire body. The form turned into the ghostly image of the old man before us and as Hakim repeated his name yet again, the second form of Gregory sat up in his bed.

I should make it clear that Gregory's wife and children remained completely unaware of what was transpiring. Their eyes continued to focus on the man laying before them. They saw not the ghostly image of him nor could they hear any of the words that were spoken. They perceived only a husband and father dying in his bed.

Hakim #60 smiled and spoke again, "Gregory . . . my name is Hakim."

The vaporous form of the old man stared in wide-eyed amazement at the towering figure before him, "Who are you?" he appeared startled.

"I am Hakim," he repeated, "I have come to offer you a position."

"What do you mean?" Gregory asked in surprise. His ghostly image looked at the giant of a man before him and then turned to view the three of us standing in wait, as well. "What is happening?"

"We work for the League," Hakim replied. "We seek your assistance in our path of great service." The tall man moved a Horologium toward the vaporous form of Gregory and added, "Should you choose to be employed in the same manner, I offer you this."

Gregory appeared surprised, "What is it?"

Hakim was matter-of-fact, "We call it a Horologium. If you choose to take this, your desire to be of service will become a reality."

Gregory looked first to his wife and daughter, and then to his sons, "What will happen to my family?"

"They will bury their father and husband, and you will become a Wayfarer. But you must decide quickly."

The ghostly image of Gregory looked again at his wife and children and then reached out to take the watch. A moment later, Hakim and the vaporous Gregory were gone.

The dying Gregory remained in his bed. His breathing became more shallow. His children could only watch.

Miriam repeated herself, "It won't be long now."

Before Ruth, George, or I could speak a word, another voice broke the silence. "Within the last few moments, I have suddenly gained a memory of you three being present for the occasion of my recruitment. What is happening?" the worn but kindly face of Gregory, the Wayfarer, was before us.

"I have come to give you a choice," Ruth said softly, "Do you wish to return to the League, or would you rather allow this to come to an end?"

Gregory moved toward us and said without any measure of regret, "Worry not. I have long desired this very moment. I choose to return to the past. It is not right for a man to live so long."

Ruth nodded, saying only, "Let me tell you what comes next."

Gregory sighed, "At last, I am done."

The activities of one individual across multiple timelines are not always consistent. Although you may find a target of influence extremely susceptible to choices in accord with your mission upon one timeline, that very same individual may behave quite differently upon another. The complications of free will coupled with the existence of innumerable timelines seeking their own prominence make the rectification of the ATL an ongoing process rather than one solitary goal.

As a Wayfarer, it is inevitable that you will have the opportunity to revisit the same experience repeatedly. Sometimes this repetition will occur on the same timeline. On occasion, you will revisit the same experience but the timeline may have changed. Regardless of where you find yourself, or the complications you encounter, or any challenges you find along the way, know that you may begin again. When all else fails, begin again.

Excerpt, "Revisiting Your Timeline Assignment," *A Time Traveler's Code of Conduct* **by Ruth #7**

SIX: Journal Entry — November 14 ATL

Before the week that followed had come to an end, Milton #71 reconvened all of us to the classroom for an overall assessment of the progress made by the teams. His initial description made it clear that although our collective efforts had provided some measure of success, they had fallen short of the initial plans. As soon as his summary remarks had concluded, Emma spoke aloud.

"You think this mission was adequate?" she sneered in disbelief. "You only learned where the rebels were not!" She shook her head in disgust.

Milton disagreed, "That is not quite true. One of the teams found Sybil . . ."

"And she got away!" Emma interrupted, peering angrily over her horn-rimmed glasses.

"Yes, she got away," Milton admitted, "but we know thus far that she is not with Emmett or Bruce. Another team found Gregory . . ."

"He got eradicated!" Agnes #23 exclaimed excitedly from the back of the room.

Ruth #7 quickly put forth her own thoughts on the matter, "It may be more accurate to suggest that he simply decided to resign from the League."

Not wanting to appear in opposition to a member of the Core, Agnes quickly conceded, "He was a good man."

Emma was disgusted, "It sounds like he would have eventually turned himself in any way."

Before she could say more, Elder Professor Grimwald interjected, "I would imagine that between Emmett's attempts to mislead us with the Alexander decoy and his efforts to create a duplicate ATL, he has found little time to pursue these remaining Wayfarers. Even with nine of us focused on just such an endeavor, it took more than a week to find two."

Milton nodded in the affirmative, "I agree. We may decide to pursue this again later. For the time being, let us simply make note of the fact that, although we are not actively seeking, we remain very interested in finding Adda, Maude, Melvin, and Sybil." He looked to the back of the room and inquired of the Governor-General, "Sara, do you have anything more to add before we disband the meeting?"

Sara nodded, grasping the arm of our instructress beside her, and said, "I just want us all to thank Agnes for her cooperation in setting aside her curriculum for this assignment. Agnes, we appreciate you." The face of our teacher filled with a smile broader than any I had witnessed before. Agnes bobbed up and down excitedly, "You are all most welcome. I would do anything for the Core and the League!"

What followed the meeting's dismissal was referred to as a "stretch break," but the intermission provided was far too short to be of any use whatsoever. There was insufficient time for a return to our chambers let alone a journey to the café for either conversation or provisions. After this brief intermission, Agnes stood before us, stylus in hand, and wrote the words "Abbeville Time Slip" on the board.

"This is another time slip account you can choose to discuss in the essay!" she reminded us enthusiastically.

My roomie, George, smiled and spoke just loud enough for me to hear, "I sure hope she gives us some background information."

Our instructress turned to glance in our direction. Apparently, she had not heard his exact words as she stated immediately thereafter, "Let me give you some background information."

She turned back to the board and used her stylus to write, "Charlie and LC." Even from the beginning of the tale, she was excited. "I will describe the same details that were included in the story when it first appeared. It happened in Louisiana, in the fall of 1969, and it is truly an amazing tale!"

Agnes bobbed about and looked repeatedly toward us as if to ascertain whether we were sufficiently engaged in the narrative.

"Now Charlie and LC were on Highway 167 near Abbeville, Louisiana—that is about 20 miles south of a place called Lafayette. They were business associates involved with selling insurance and had just finished lunch — I should make it clear that Charlie was driving and LC was on the passenger side."

Agnes gripped an imaginary wheel before her and began to drive about the front of the classroom, providing us with a theatrical component to her description.

"They saw no other cars on the highway but one."

Suddenly, both her movements and her driving stopped. She squinted her eyes as if to perceive some vehicle way off in the distance.

"They saw a car up ahead of them that was moving much too slowly for the highway. Charlie drove his own car to catch up with the vehicle and then slowed behind it. The two men were astonished!" Agnes slapped the top of her desk, and added, "The car was decades old but appeared in perfect condition. It had one of those turtleback trunks like an old DeSoto or Packard. LC pointed out that it had a bright orange license plate with the date 1940 clearly visible. Now in 1969, the standard Louisiana plate was light green. LC commented that such a plate was probably not even legal on the highway."

Her narration continued, "Both cars were going about 25 miles per hour. Charlie pulled up beside the antique car on its left, giving LC a perfect view of the car's occupants. The driver was a young woman in her late twenties or early thirties. She wore 1940s clothing with a feathered hat and a fur coat. Next to the driver was a small child wearing a heavy coat and cap. LC thought their attire was most unusual as the day was not even cold. When the woman turned and looked at the two men, LC observed that she appeared horrified."

Agnes waved the stylus at each of us in turn, "The woman was frightened! She looked at the car that the two men were driving and became even more distraught. LC said that she appeared as if she was about to cry. Charlie drove alongside her for quite some time and LC commented that she was frantic. He told Charlie that he thought the woman needed help."

Agnes used her free arm to pretend that she was rolling down the car window, describing what came next.

"LC rolled down his window and yelled out, 'Do you need help?' The young woman nodded, and LC motioned with his hands for her to pull over to the side of the road. The woman slowed her own car and merged onto the shoulder of the road on the right. Charlie slowed his car, passed the woman and her child, and pulled over to the side of the road in front of the antique car. LC and Charlie turned to look through the back window at the occupants behind them. At that very moment, the car vanished."

Agnes stood still.

"The two men were astonished! They got out of their vehicle and looked in every direction. Suddenly a third car pulled up behind them. A businessman wearing a suit and tie jumped out and demanded, 'Did you see that?' He, too, was dumbfounded having just witnessed the antique car pull off to the side of the highway and disappear."

"The three discussed what each of them had seen and then looked along the dirt shoulder for any evidence of the old car's tire tracks. The businessman wanted them to drive back into Abbeville and report the incident to the police. He suggested they file a missing person's report. LC and Charlie disagreed, insisting that no one would believe them. What they had seen was preposterous to anyone who had not witnessed it firsthand. Reporting the sudden disappearance of a 1940s woman, child, and automobile to the authorities would call their own sanity into question. In the end, the three exchanged phone numbers with one another. Over the next few years, they checked in on two or three occasions simply to confirm the story between them."

Agnes slapped the top of her desk for a second time and stated, "That is the Abbeville time slip. It is truly a remarkable tale!"

It was my roomie, George, who raised his hand into the air and inquired before being called upon, "Miss Agnes, what happened to the woman and her child?"

For an instant, our instructress seemed perplexed by the query, but after a moment she demanded, "Why does that even matter?"

George was undeterred, "It is a crucial part of the story. We know what happened to all of the others who were involved in one of these time slip experiences."

Manuela #64 agreed aloud with George, "I would be most interested in knowing the outcome for this woman and her child."

Our teacher shook her head in indifference, "I do not see how this is relevant to the time slip."

Bonne Soeur Marie interjected, "Perhaps we could find an answer in the Akasha Library?"

Agnes was undeterred, "Perhaps," she conceded, "but since we don't know the names of either the woman or her child, finding the answer might be a real needle in a haystack." She looked out upon the class, seemingly readying herself for another comment on the matter. When there was none, she turned toward my roomie, "George #111, why don't you read for us where we left off in Chapter 6, 'Revisiting Your Timeline Assignment?'"

Later that day, after class had been dismissed, the five of us journeyed to the Akasha in search of Athena and an answer to George's query. We gathered around a library table and listened as my roomie retold the Abbeville tale before inquiring how we might discover what happened to the woman and her child after the time slip. Through it all, my sweetheart listened attentively. However, before Athena could respond, George had more to say.

"We have been told repeatedly that everything happens for a reason. What was the reason for the Abbeville time slip anyway?" His query sounded like a challenge.

Athena twirled a strand of her dark hair between two fingers, appearing totally unflustered by the question, "Are you interested in what happened in Abbeville or how everything happens for a reason?"

George's response was immediate, "Both."

Athena nodded, "You understand that the fundamental purpose of the Prime Directive is the pursuit of what is best for the Whole?"

My roomie's response was simply, "In theory."

"Can you accept the idea that even when bad things happen, good can come as a result?"

George was not to be swayed, "It would truly depend on the circumstance."

Athena was undeterred, "Let me suggest that the potential for good is always present. Always, George," she repeated. "It is an individual's freedom of choice that determines whether that good comes as a result."

"How can a personal tragedy lead to good?" George asked.

"I can give you many, many examples. People often use misfortune as a learning process and become changed because of the event. Countless individuals have used a personal tragedy as the motivation to help others through a similar experience."

Hoping to assist my beloved, I interjected, "Athena, perhaps you could provide an example?"

"Absolutely," Athena replied, "in the collective illusion of 1880, a healthy baby girl was born to a husband and wife in Alabama. Before the child was two years old, she contracted scarlet fever, which left her deaf and blind. The girl's parents were devastated. For the next five years, that child was unable to communicate or understand the world in which she lived. The family sought help, only to go through one disappointment after another. The girl's mother eventually found her daughter a teacher and mentor, who was able to teach the child to read braille. By the time their daughter was 14, she could speak clearly enough to be understood. She eventually entered college and graduated at the top of her class. She became an advocate for the blind and deaf and wrote countless articles and more than a dozen books. She became an international speaker and even helped to organize the American Civil Liberties Union. At the age of 84, she was awarded the Presidential Medal of Freedom. In spite of the tremendous hardship that had been thrust upon her as a child, her life would have a lasting influence on the lives of millions. Her name was Helen Keller."

George pondered her words for a few moments and then inquired, "What about a tragedy that affects hundreds or thousands, or even an entire country? How can good come of such disaster?"

Athena was quick to respond, "Throughout history, individuals have often joined together to create positive change even in the face of immense difficulties. Life is not created by what happens to us, George. Life comes as a result of how we choose to respond to what happens." Athena twirled a few strands of hair as she appeared to draw upon her knowledge of the Akasha. "In ancient Rome, the rape of Lucretia, a noblewoman, led to the uprising of regular citizens, the end of the Roman monarchy, and the creation of a democratic republic. During the Middle Ages, the plague of the Black Death killed one-third of Europe, but out of the devastation came vast changes to society, culture, and religion, and the Renaissance was born. During World War I, as men were drawn into the war, women took their place at work, taking jobs that had never been available to them before. As a result, in less than a decade, they gained the right to vote. George, the list goes on and on."

Bonne Soeur Marie voiced her hope from earlier that day, "We were wondering whether the records might indicate what happened to this woman and her child in Abbeville. Is this possible?"

"It is possible," Athena concurred, "but it depends on whether the two told anyone else about their experience, or whether that event created a major change in their lives. Let me do some research, and I will be right back." Athena smiled at me before departing down one of the book corridors.

"She is amazing!" Manuela affirmed, prompting a smile upon my face.

However, the smile quickly disappeared as the sound of a woman's angry voice interrupted, "Shouldn't you all be in class?"

I turned to see Emma #119 standing before us. She glared with irritation as she peered over her black spectacles, shaking her head in disgust, "Surely there is something more constructive you could all be doing?"

It was Emanuel who responded, "Madame, we are here for a follow-up class discussion."

Emma was unmoved, "Really?" her response sounded skeptical.

Silence followed, prompting Bonne Soeur Marie to nervously comment, "We heard you were becoming a Wayfarer in the field?"

Emma's voice filled with disgust, "I wouldn't count on it." She shook her head in defiance, turned, and departed down one of the rows of books.

George stated the obvious, "She is definitely not happy."

A moment later, Athena returned to the table holding one of the Akasha volumes in her hand. "I found an answer but it's not the one you were looking for."

My roomie repeated his earlier inquiry, "What was the reason for the Abbeville time slip?"

She placed the book on the table before us, opened it, and turned several pages as she informed the five of us, "It would appear that neither the woman nor her child ever revealed the incident to anyone. I found no record mentioning either one of them."

Bonne Soeur Marie pondered aloud, "Perhaps they were afraid of what others might think?"

"So why did it happen?" George restated.

Athena pointed to a section of the volume on the table, "It seems the event became life-changing for Charlie, the man driving the car."

"In what way?" I could not help but inquire.

Athena responded with certainty, "You can read it all for yourselves if you want but it is evident that before the experience Charlie lived a life without faith, without wonder, without the conjecture that there may be much more to the human condition than simply the physical world." She smiled, "The Abbeville time slip changed all that completely."

Toward day's end, we all gathered at the League Café for supper. I chose a small serving of sliced turkey and cranberries and thereafter selected one of the larger tables so that I could save the chair next to me for Athena. (She expected to finish her work in the library at any moment.) George's partiality for curry and potatoes had prompted him to choose such fare for his own plate, and he sat across from me. My Swede friend's immense fondness for vegetables and rolls induced him to place such on the platter before him. And, as I recall, both Manuela and Soeur Marie had selected the pork dish and rice for their evening repast.

Emanuel raised his glass before us, "To friendship and useful labors, and the meal before us."

We heartily agreed and began to dine and converse amongst ourselves. It was Bonne Soeur Marie who commented on Athena's findings from earlier that day.

"What we learned in the Akasha this afternoon was très intéressant . . . very interesting. I was very surprised to hear about Charlie."

I concurred, "The Akasha has all of the knowledge you could ever hope to possess. It is the most amazing library."

George nodded his agreement.

Manuela #64 exclaimed, "For me, I was most taken by Athena's explanation of how we shape our lives. I have repeated her words all afternoon, 'Life is not created by what happens to us; life comes as a result of how we choose to respond to what happens.'"

"Such a philosophy should prompt one to act in

accordance with reason," Emanuel #41 interjected. I could not help but wonder whether the discussion had influenced my roomie in any way, "George, what are your thoughts on the matter? Do you think that good might arise from any circumstance?"

George placed his fork on his plate and contemplated the question for a moment. Nonetheless, the response which came forth was no different from what he had voiced earlier, "It would depend on the circumstance."

I continued, "So you were not swayed in the least by Athena's comments?"

"I believe I have been quite clear on the matter. It depends on the circumstance."

"I see." I quickly recalled one of our discussions from earlier in the semester that seemed most appropriate for the occasion, "Do you remember after we first met? You told me about your experience distributing coins worth half a crown to the poor in London."

"Go on." George waved his fork in my direction.

"You said that most often when you placed the coin within a palm, the individual behaved as though you had provided a fortune. However, on a few occasions, the recipient behaved quite differently, becoming angry because you appeared as one who could have given so much more."

"And how is this relevant to our present discussion?"

"Did we not conclude at the time that an individual's perception of a situation helped to create their experience of it?"

Emanuel and Bonne Soeur Marie both nodded while my roomie stared quietly at his supper before him. After a period of silence, George reluctantly agreed, "I may need to give this additional consideration . . ."

"Mon chéri, Ben!" A French woman's voice interrupted our conversation. I turned to see Louise

#217 standing behind the empty chair that I had saved for Athena. She placed her plate on the table and quickly sat in the chair beside me.

Although taken by surprise, I immediately told her, "I am sorry, Louise, I am saving that for Athena."

"Well, my dear," Louise spoke assertively, "she is not here. I can see no Athena." She looked around the café, shaking her head in the negative, and then turned her smile toward each of the faces before her. "I do not wish to interrupt this discussion, please continue." She smiled, winking her blue eyes as she glanced in my direction. I could not help but notice how the overhead lights of the café caused her skin to glisten.

My roomie appeared very much relieved that he was no longer the central focus of discussion. He turned to Louise and inquired, "How are things in the ATL Mission Office? Do you have our next assignments?"

Louise was cheerful, "Things are just wonderful! And most certainly, we have gathered your assignments, but Ms. Agnes would not be pleased with me if I were to discuss such things with you before she was able. You will discover soon enough."

Suddenly, I felt a firm hand squeeze my shoulder from behind, "Hello everyone," Athena's voice sounded normal and then became louder, "Hello, Louise!"

I rose to embrace my sweetheart with more passion than I had previously demonstrated within the confines of the café.

After Athena and I had embraced, Louise used her fork to point to a couple of empty chairs at the other end of the table, "I believe those seats are still available," she said sweetly.

"I am going to sit next to my boyfriend," Athena was quick to respond. I could not help but notice how she tugged on the strands of hair much harder than usual.

"I think Ben was saving that seat for me."

Louise shrugged, "Perhaps, but did the poet not say, 'All is fair in love?'"

"And war," George added quietly.

Before another word could be spoken, I took both my plate and Athena's in hand and moved us toward the empty chairs at the other end of the table.

The next morning, after we had all taken our seats, Agnes stood at the front of the classroom with stylus in one hand and several pieces of paper in the other. She waved the stylus before us, exclaiming with some measure of satisfaction, "I am sure you will all be very pleased to learn that I have your most recent assignments from the ATL Mission Office!" She bobbed about for only a moment before coming to a stop.

She exclaimed, "Do not take as long on these new assignments as you did on the last ones. Understood?" She looked about the room, making certain she had eye contact with each of us in turn. When she had our complete attention, she turned to read the pages within her hand.

"Ben #239, destination Mali, Africa, 1236, in the matter of the Manden Charter, addressing human rights."

She handed several pages to me.

"Bonne Soeur Marie #304, destination Basel, Switzerland, 1527, in the matter of preventing Paracelsus from being evicted from the city.

After Soeur Marie received her assignment, Emanuel was next.

"Emanuel #41, destination Yazlovets, Ukraine, 1717, in the matter of Rabbi Israel ben Eliezer and the establishment of Hasidism.

George followed.

"George #111, destination Sydney, Australia, 1821, in the matter of Samuel Terry's philanthropy."

Agnes handed the remaining mission to Manuela.

"Manuela #64, destination Tacoma and Port Townsend, Washington, 1890s, in the matter of Thomas and William Bishop and their advocacy for the Snohomish Indians."

Her final advice was her usual.

"This afternoon, I recommend you visit the Akasha and research whatever additional information you might need for these assignments. Use your time wisely! If you need help, ask Athena."

As soon as her words were spoken, something caused George to look at the doorway, prompting me to turn in the same direction. Sara #11, Ruth #7, Milton #71, and my own Athena stood before us. It was the Governor-General who spoke.

"Please excuse the interruption, Agnes."

Her voice startled our instructress who jumped and then responded with, "Ms. Sara? What can we do for you this morning?"

"We have a problem," Sara replied as the four entered the room.

"What problem?"

Sara turned to Milton and inquired, "Will you tell them?"

"I will," his response was somber. "As you know, earlier both Athena and I came across a shadow of a timeline—an alternate to the ATL that was faint and ephemeral but appeared to be an alternate history dealing with Alexander the Great . . ."

Bonne Soeur Marie interrupted, "And Monsieur Ben and I undertook a background mission for information, and later Ben returned to address this problem."

"Yes," Milton continued, "and it became very clear that Emmett had created a decoy for us. However, a little while ago, I was doing some research in the Akasha for upcoming Wayfarer missions and decided to watch for myself the outcome of Ben's efforts . . ."

Agnes interrupted, "What did you see?"

"I came across the same shadow of a timeline I had seen earlier, only this time it was more pronounced. It was not as faded or as ephemeral as it appeared earlier. It remained in place for so long that not only was I able to show Athena but Sara and Ruth saw it as well."

Emanuel voiced my own thoughts on the matter, "What does this mean? Was the decoy not really a decoy?"

"It was a decoy, but it appears that Emmett gave us the decoy to keep us focused and occupied while he continues his own efforts creating an alternate version of the very same period in history."

George responded, "I do not understand."

Milton turned to Ruth #7, "Can you tell them what you told us?"

Ruth nodded and explained it, as follows, "Think of it this way. There are innumerable timelines. Some are of little importance and will never come to the attention of the League. We only become aware of a timeline when it is vying for prominence with the ATL or if it is creating an alternate to what the Core has authorized . . ."

"Isn't that what Emmett is doing?" Manuela inquired.

"Not exactly," came Ruth's response. "It would appear that Emmett has chosen a timeline very close to the actual ATL. I believe he is changing that timeline to become an exact duplicate of the one approved by the

Core. Once that happens, it could take prominence over our own and if that occurs any changes he decides to make will become the approved ATL."

"How can we discover which timeline Emmett is changing?" I inquired.

Milton responded, "That is a question for which we do not yet have an answer. There are potentially hundreds, if not more. Once we decide on the proper course of action, we may need to send some of you to investigate further."

The Governor-General turned to our teacher, "Obviously, any background mission to explore what Emmett is doing will need to take precedence over the curriculum."

Agnes nodded as she replied, "He needs to be eradicated."

In the beginning, it may be surprising to contemplate the fact that the one tool you used most often prior to your recruitment into the League has become the very tool without meaning whatsoever. That tool is time. When you were part of the Collective Illusion it was the instrument that guided your schedule, coordinated your every event, recorded your past, and even planned for your future. Almost everything with which you were involved was regulated by the parameter of time.

Ultimately, you will come to the realization that time is without meaning. It has no capacity to control consciousness, to defeat Wholeness, or to sway the self in one direction or another. It is nothing more than an illusory instrument of the physical world. To be sure, one has the capacity to give it power, strength, or meaning but these things are only temporary. When compared to the limitless manifestation of NOW, time is nothing more than a passing figment of personal perception.

Excerpt, "The Limitless Expression of Time," *A Time Traveler's Code of Conduct* by Ruth #7

SEVEN: Journal Entry — November 20 ATL

In spite of the immense concern regarding Emmett's alternate timeline, until a course of action was agreed upon by the Governor-General and those surrounding her, our classwork continued in accord with Agnes's chosen schedule. From brief conversations with my sweetheart, I understood that members of the Core had been meeting regularly or had at least been communicating their thoughts from the field. The overreaching problem was that it was seemingly impossible for a small group of individuals to explore literally hundreds of potential timelines. Although it was apparent that Emmett planned to alter the history of Alexander, the League had no way of knowing which timeline he was changing to create a duplicate of the ATL.

Regardless of the threat posed by the situation, I must admit that I found the classroom discussion dealing with the scientific perspective of time to be most intriguing. Agnes #23 used her stylus to write the name, "Albert Einstein" on the board as well as the words, "Space-Time," "Gravity," and "Motion." She underscored each of the words twice over and assured us all that we would be fascinated by her discussion of the "scientific nature of time." She reminded the class, "Some of this will be included in the final exam!"

For the hour that ensued, we were provided with "sufficient background information" regarding this Mr. Einstein. He was a German-born scientist employed as a clerk in a Swiss patent office who immigrated to the United States and eventually became known as one of the most notable physicists in history. Although he had apparently made major contributions to a number of scientific fields, Agnes placed her focus on Einstein's work regarding the subject of time.

"Einstein proposed that time is affected by gravity and motion!" she said with more enthusiasm than appeared necessary for such a statement. She slapped her free hand upon the desktop and exclaimed, "In other words, time is not a constant!"

Our instructress turned to the board and drew what she called "a rocket ship" to illustrate this point. She drew a little figure she labeled "an astronaut" at the top end of the rocket ship and a similar astronaut figure at the base of the vehicle. She continued, "Let us imagine that this is a picture of an accelerating rocket ship that is so long it takes light one second to travel from the astronaut at the top of the rocket to the astronaut near the engines at the bottom. Let us also imagine that this astronaut at the top of the rocket is told to flash a bright light once every second, and the other astronaut is told to record how often that light signal is observed."

She whipped around and inquired of the class, "Is that clear?" She found herself greeted only by silence, prompting her to continue.

"Because this rocket is accelerating through space so quickly, the first flashing light from the astronaut at the top will be seen by the second astronaut in less than one second. And the next time the light flashes, it will be seen even sooner. Even though the first astronaut is flashing the light only once every second, the other astronaut will begin seeing these flashing lights much more quickly as the rocket ship accelerates through space. Obviously, this demonstrates how motion affects the passage of time. Surely, this is clear?"

Whether or not any of us had some semblance of clarity, no one chose to respond. The silence was encouraging enough for the instruction to resume.

"Einstein also suggested that time and space are linked. He called this connection 'space-time' and said that space-time could be warped by gravity." She took the stylus and drew a circle on the board and labeled it "Bowling Ball," and proceeded. "Imagine this bowling ball is like a planet with a gravitational field around it." She then drew a line that was straight until it came to the bowling ball, where she chose instead to outline the underside of the bowling ball before us. She labeled this line "Blanket."

"Imagine that space-time is like a blanket. If you placed this bowling ball upon a blanket on your bed, the blanket would become curved or warped, following the outline of the heavy ball. This is exactly how space-time is warped by gravity. Surely, that is clear?"

It was George who finally chose to respond to her query, "Aren't both space and time essentially nothing more than an illusion?"

"Yes," Agnes replied quickly.

My roomie was confused, "Then what is the purpose of this discussion?"

Our instructress shook her head in frustration, "Because we are talking about science! Even science disagrees with the perspective of time held in mind by most of those crippled by the Collective Illusion! Both time and space are very different than what people imagine!"

Our teacher returned to the curriculum, "All you will need to remember is that gravity causes the passage of time to slow down." Agnes nodded in response to her own statement and then added, "Obviously, this is why black holes in space have such an impact upon the illusion of time!"

"What?" George inquired.

Bonne Soeur Marie raised her hand and stated what was true for us all, "Madame, I have not heard of this black hole before."

Agnes took a cloth to wipe the picture of her bowling ball from the board and wrote instead the words "Black Hole," which were appropriately underlined.

"A black hole is a place in space where gravity is so strong that nothing—not even light—can escape from it . . ." She paused. "You know," she pondered aloud as she pointed back to the board, "according to the Schwarzchild time dilation theory, if our astronauts in that rocket were able to fly near a black hole for one year, more than 100 years would have passed on earth . . ."

"What?" George repeated.

Emanuel voiced his own concern, "Surely this will not be included as part of the examination?"

Agnes looked out upon the stares of confusion before her, sighed, and finally agreed, "The final only deals with the topic of Einstein and how the illusion of time can be impacted by both gravity and motion. We will have the opportunity to discuss this topic further . . . after graduation."

I found myself very much confused, "There is another class after graduation?"

"Of course!" Agnes responded as though my query was most unusual. "Every Wayfarer is required to take continuing education. It is part of your ongoing certification. I teach a graduate seminar two evenings each week."

George turned to me and groaned, "You have got to be kidding."

While I resided in Philadelphia, I gained respect and admiration for much that the Native American way of life had to offer. The American Indians chose to govern themselves through the wise counsel of elders and sages. They used no force to control their people nor did they find the need for prisons. Both men and women remained industrious throughout their lives as a means of addressing what few needs they possessed. They appeared to want very little, providing them with sufficient time for leisure and conversation. By comparison, so much of what we valued within the colonies seemed useless and frivolous.

Perhaps it was my overall admiration of the Indian that prompted me to be very interested in Manuela's report detailing her most recent time travel mission. Our Latin classmate stood before her peers and began by writing the names "Thomas Bishop" and "William Bishop" on the board before us. As was her usual approach with these oral reports, she provided adequate background material for our overall comprehension of the assignment. From the beginning, she made it quite clear that the purpose of the assignment she had been given by the ATL Mission Office was limited.

"I wish I could say that my efforts were instrumental in helping to solve all problems for the Snohomish tribe but that is not the case."

Manuela #64 proceeded to inform us that Thomas and William had been born to a Snohomish woman and a British sailor, and the two had settled near the shores of the Salish Sea. The sea was bordered by British Columbia to the north and what would become the state of Washington to the south. The children grew up among Indian elders who remembered the Hudson Bay trading posts and the humiliation of Native peoples who were forced to sign one treaty after another. The United States prohibited Indian self-rule because of an 1831 court case that determined "an American Indian tribe does not exist as a legal entity unless the federal government decides that it exists."

I should note herein that when Manuela advised us of this fact, Agnes #23 shook her head in disgust (making some semblance of appropriate notation within her ledger).

According to Manuela, "My mission assignment with each brother proved to be quite different. In the case of William, the younger brother by two years, he became a successful businessman, eventually relocated to Port Townsend, Washington, and made a name for himself in real estate and farming. He also established a creamery that employed many locals. It was his talent as a businessman that would become my challenge on multiple timelines."

She went on to describe how his business success on timelines CCCXIX and LXIII especially were vying for prominence with the ATL and threatened to keep him from any political involvement. Apparently, the Akasha indicated that William's participation in politics was instrumental to the approved timeline. Manuela went on to discuss how on numerous occasions she had witnessed William's tremendous speaking abilities in front of other businessmen. It was his talent for public speaking where she placed her influence.

She smiled, "In local newspapers, William's ability to capture the attention of an audience would become known as 'spellbinding.'"

It was this gift she used to bring him to the attention of local politics. At first, he gave talks only to businessmen; later, the numbers and background of his audiences grew. Although William always maintained some involvement in his farm and business, Manuela's influence on the competing timelines led to William's involvement in Washington State politics.

"For the next 35 years, he became a major influence in both the state House and Senate. His political experience helped him to draft the Snohomish Tribe Constitution in 1926. He also made certain to have it legally incorporated the following year. William Bishop would even serve as its first legal president."

When she had completed her discussion of William, she went on to describe how his younger brother, Thomas, moved to a place called Tacoma—a thriving city with more than 80,000 residents. There he found work in a meat shop and eventually saved enough to purchase his own confectionary store.

Manuela was quick to inform us, "Within a few years, his store burned to the ground in an unexplained fire."

Regardless of whether the fire was due to arson or an accident, on multiple timelines it had prompted Thomas to move his family out of Tacoma. Such an outcome was in opposition to the approved timeline, creating multiple problems for the ATL. Manuela decided that the best way to keep him in Tacoma was to make him more aware of the many issues facing his Native people.

"I also encouraged him to rebuild the candy store, no matter the cost."

Through Manuela's efforts, Thomas became very much aware and troubled by the fate of Indians who had been driven from their Native lands. Many of his people had lost their ancestral property as well as their hunting and fishing rights. He organized ongoing meetings for "landless Indians" and helped to create the Society of American Indians. He eventually became president of the National Federal of Indians and championed the importance of gathering the Native stories and traditions of the elders so that they could be passed down to future generations. "He interviewed countless Native elders from the Salish coast so that their memories of the past would be preserved. Later, it was said that 'history could have died' without him."

She concluded her report with, "Thomas died in 1923, and William eleven years later. In 1924, American Indians were finally given United States citizenship just as Thomas Bishop had been supporting for years. Although the government kept complete control over Indian reservations for another ten years, in 1934 Congress decided to slowly delegate authority back to the Indians. It finally happened in total in 1975, when the Indian right to self-govern was recognized. The year before, Native fishing rights had also been reconfirmed once and for all."

Manuela's final thought on the assignment prompted us to applaud in recognition of her efforts. "The work of the Bishop brothers would have a lasting impact upon their Native people even long after they had died."

Once she had completed her report, Emanuel #41 came next. His assignment proved most straightforward. Our Swede friend explained how the timeline problem had occurred because of the death of the young wife of his target, Israel ben Eliezer. The young man had lost her within the first year of their marriage, causing him immense sadness. Once she died, his focus turned solely to his occupation: the law, mediation, and helping the less fortunate. To be sure, such a response enabled him to deal with the tragedy. Unfortunately, it also became problematic, as the ATL indicated a much greater destiny.

Emanuel used his influence to arrange for an encounter between Israel ben Eliezer and a Rabbi versed in the Jewish Mysticism of the Kabbalah. The meeting became life changing. It caused Israel to begin a lifelong pursuit of the divine. He began searching for the Creator within every waking moment and every human interaction. It was a motivation that eventually gained a following. He turned to teaching others what he had come to learn and became known as "the Besht" ("one with a good reputation"). He was the founder of Hasidic Judaism, and created a way of life for countless others.

After exploring the life of one involved in such spiritual pursuits, it was somewhat ironic to have my roomie's report on Samuel Terry follow.

Terry was an individual who seemed devoid of any

moral principles, whatsoever. According to George, he arrived in Australia in chains, having been convicted of thievery in Manchester, England. During the seven years of imprisonment that followed, Terry labored as a stonemason on behalf of the colony. When his sentence ended, he changed his luck by marrying the widow of another convict—a woman named Rosetta Marsh, who owned the Pitt Street Inn. Terry made a name for himself by threatening businessmen, extorting other property owners, and strong-arming lucrative supply deals with the government. Within a decade, he was the owner of 19,000 acres and held the mortgages on more than 20 percent of property within the state. He was also the largest shareholder in the Bank of New South Wales and had become Australia's richest man ever—worth billions many times over.

George explained, "Even though Terry's life lacked all manner of human charity on several timelines, the ATL foresaw a more positive potential."

He explained his chosen course of action, "I witnessed how Terry's upbringing had rarely given him the benefit of any system of personal morality. As he grew older, he was unable to benefit from the camaraderie and mutual support of others. I called to mind my own experience in Freemasonry, and decided the Masons might be the very tool needed to rectify the timeline."

Obviously, the statement prompted me to take note, as I had greatly benefited from my own involvement in Freemasonry and had even arranged for the first Masonic book to be printed in Philadelphia.

My roomie continued, "The Masonic Lodge proved to be his moral salvation and the basis of his transformation. He went through the orders of the lodge, enjoyed the company and support of others, experienced a rebirth, and even became lodge president in 1826. He began contributing his money to schools, to the city, and to the needs of many others. The focus of his final years was on helping people. He even worked for the benefit of convicts, enabling others to turn their lives around. Before his death, he became known as Australia's greatest philanthropist."

When he finished his report, I eagerly anticipated a trip to the League Café for some much-needed refreshment. Before a word could be uttered regarding such a possibility, however, Agnes #23 arrived at the front of the class, thanked George for his efforts, and was quick to inform us what was next on the schedule.

"Before the break, we need to take time for another class review. Our final will be here before you know it!"

With the exception of our instructress, it became exceedingly clear no one present was enthused in the least by such an agenda.

As I recall, it was that very evening (or the one thereafter) in which Athena and I finally found occasion to come together for some private time within her chambers. The room was cast in shadows, possessing only some semblance of illumination put off by the light on her bedtable. In spite of much familiarity between us, our passion for one another had not abated in the least. In fact, the infrequency with which we were able to pursue such sport of late was only due to the demands of school on my part, and the never-ending schedule of research on her own. I kissed her lips a final time and smiled at her beauty once more before moving aside, turning on my back, and staring at the ceiling in complete satisfaction.

"You are most amazing," I sighed aloud.

She reached out and squeezed my hand. "I have missed you. I do not like it when our schedules keep us apart."

I agreed and voiced those things which had been pondered earlier within my mind, "In little more than a fortnight, school will come to an end. Although my classes will be over, I remain most certain that a Wayfarer's schedule keeps oneself quite occupied. In light of the Emmett situation, I do not foresee a prevalence of leisure time for either one of us."

"I think you are right," Athena said softly. "We will have to find ways to make time between us."

I affirmed, "Let us vow to do just that. By the by, you told me Milton still required your assistance in pulling together these mission overviews for Wayfarers in the field. Can you not acquire an assistant to help with such matters?"

"I remain hopeful that the demands on my time will diminish."

"It appears you are responsible for the research of far too many mission assignments. Does the ATL Mission Office have ongoing communications with every Wayfarer in the field?"

Athena only stated, "It does."

I queried, "Does that suggest that the ATL Mission Office knows where every Wayfarer is located?"

She paused for a moment before responding, "No. There are far too many timelines within the Collective Illusion. A Horologium is capable of receiving all communication sent out from the League but its location is unknown unless its user impacts the timeline . . . Why?"

"So the League could get a message to Emmett, even if we don't know where he is?"

"It could send the message, but whether or not he chooses to listen would be up to Emmett."

I furthered my query, "How many Wayfarers in the field does the ATL Mission Office oversee?"

"I can't tell you that!" The answer came quickly. "There are certain things that should not be spoken between us."

I paused for only a moment before inquiring, "If I were to provide you with a number, would you tell me whether or not my estimate was close?"

"I would not."

I could not help but smile. "Never mind. It just seems that you have sufficient work to keep more than one individual sufficiently engaged. Perhaps an assistant would give you more time for yourself?"

"I remain hopeful that Louise #217 will soon be able to take on even more of the research I have been doing."

At the mention of Louise, silence arose between us. Finally, after too many moments of quiet, Athena inquired, "Do you think Louise is attractive?"

I considered my best response before finally speaking, "I fear such a question does not have a suitable answer."

Her hand pulled away from me, "Why not?"

I sighed, "If I say no, you will not believe me. If I say yes, you will become angry."

She pondered my words before replying with some measure of frustration, "So you do find her attractive?"

I cleared my throat, sighed, and chose to reply, "Like yourself, I find that there are certain things that should not be spoken between us."

Agnes's insistence that these latest missions were to be accomplished "without delay whatsoever" had prompted each of us to place a primary focus in that very direction. Although I had pledged to follow through and undertake my latest timeline assignment as swiftly as possible, I became the last to journey beyond the confines of the League school for that very undertaking. In the end, Bonne Soeur Marie and I would be the final two making our classroom reports.

To be sure, my delay was not due to idleness. Aside from class time and never-ending "required homework assignments" and two trips to the Akasha in search of background information, there were numerous occasions when I found myself speaking with and reassuring Athena about the Louise situation. Although I cannot state with certainty that my sweetheart moved completely beyond the issue, I was grateful to observe a wink cast in my direction just prior to my departure for the African assignment.

Let me note from the onset that the Akasha Library proved most illuminating regarding this matter of the Manden Charter. During my younger years, I had sufficiently educated myself to be conversant on the Magna Carta — the charter of rights signed into law by King John. I must admit total ignorance, however, in understanding that the ruler of the Mali Empire, Sundiata Keita, had created an oral charter of human rights as a contemporary of Britain's own.

Accessing the unlimited information available within the Akasha, one can certainly gather more information than necessary for the successful completion of these mission assignments. Undoubtedly, I have repeatedly erred on the side of possessing much more insight than I needed. (I will note, however, that this has frequently proven advantageous during the "oral reports" that Agnes demands.) With that in mind, I choose to include herein only that which is necessary to provide a highlight of my experience in Africa.

Sundiata Keita would become one of the most important leaders in all of African history. Although he began only as the ruler of a small local tribe, he quickly rose to prominence when he championed other tribes to join with him in opposition to trade restrictions imposed upon them by the empire of Ghana. The revolt succeeded and afterwards Keita united the surrounding kingdoms to form the Mali Empire. In time, it would grow to become one of the richest kingdoms in the world and a center for African and Arab trade. Keita became known as "the Lion King."

According to the Akasha, it was the coming together of the African and Arab religions that became problematic for the stability of the ATL. The Arab world desired to deal only with a ruler who was Islamic like themselves; the African tribes wished their ruler to ascribe to the beliefs of their ancestors. It was this very conflict that led to Keita's defeat (or death) on multiple timelines.

I originally considered such a mission perhaps more suitable for Emanuel's area of expertise and resolution, but it quickly became apparent that what was needed most was diplomacy. I used my influence to assist Keita in those very things where he was already quite adept: mediation, tact, and all manner of subtlety. By so doing, Arab traders became convinced that Keita had converted to their faith, as Keita subscribed to the five pillars of Islam and became well-versed in the Quran. The African people were just as convinced that Keita had not abandoned the faith of his forefathers and remained totally devoted to the African religion. Because he was able to interact and deal with all manner of people, some called him a peacemaker, others a magician. With such a resolution, Keita governed in peace, and the kingdom became the focus of much commerce and trade — gold, salt, rice, and multi-colored fabrics of every description. To be sure, Keita never voiced his own personal beliefs. He was a skilled administrator and negotiator and fulfilled the destiny foreseen for him within the ATL, giving life to the Manden Charter. It is an oral tradition of human rights that speaks to peace, the sanctity of life, women's rights, education, the abolition of slavery, the importance of food security, and the right to self-expression. Rather than choosing to provide excessive details regarding my experience with the king, it may be most noteworthy to describe what transpired as my mission neared its end.

I found myself standing within Keita's personal chambers, watching the colorfully clothed ruler discuss with his sons the duties of a king toward his people. Suddenly, I was completely startled by the sound of a loud, older voice speaking my name from behind.

"Hello, Ben."

I jumped, immediately turning around to view the old Keeper of the Records standing before me.

My response was quick, "Emmett? What are you doing here? How did you know where to find me?"

Neither Keita nor his sons became aware of the two vaporous forms within the king's chamber. Emmett glanced only once in their direction before continuing.

"My dear friend," he replied somberly, "surely, it would not surprise you to learn that I have a number of ways to determine what you and other members of the League have been doing?"

I stared inquisitively, wondering who from the League

might be helping him.

He added, "Before my departure, I decided it might become advantageous at some point to speak with you. For that reason, I looked into the Akasha, viewing for myself a number of your upcoming mission assignments. This is simply one of them."

I was intrigued, "The Akasha already contains everything that will ever occur?"

He shook his head in the negative, "Absolutely not. Every choice and every interaction has a potential impact upon a timeline. Until that choice is made, however, possible futures remain unwritten." He eyed me closely, "Were it not so, I could have seen the League's disruption of the Alexander situation. However, once a choice is made, a future's certainty becomes more stable."

"Why are you creating an alternate timeline?"

"The question answers itself," came his reply. "Surely there is an alternative to the never-ending process with which the Core has been involved."

I challenged, "We are making progress."

Emmett shook his head again, and sighed, "Really? I thought much the same throughout so many millennia." He eyed me again, "You could never imagine how many missions I researched or undertook for myself. I was there from the very first—from the beginning. The League involves itself in an endeavor without end, towards a goal that moves ever further away."

"Why are you here?"

Emmett smiled, "I could use the skills of a diplomat. Would you consider joining our work?"

I was quick to shake my head, "No. To do so, would be a mistake. I cannot see your work as anything but an act of selfishness."

At that moment, Keita and his sons departed the royal chamber, leaving the two of us alone.

He chuckled, "Selfishness? How do you arrive at such a conclusion?"

I eyed him in return, "For whom are you creating the timeline other than yourself?"

"The timeline is for any who wishes to become part of it."

"I decline the offer."

Emmett pondered my words for a moment, "Very well. Perhaps you will change your mind in the future."

"I don't think so."

Emmett was undeterred, "Nonetheless, I will check in on you again." He paused and then added, "I must say I was most intrigued by what happened on your Eleanor Roosevelt mission. It was the first time I have witnessed such an occurrence."

I was quick to reply, "I am unfamiliar with either the name or the assignment."

Emmett was clear, "It is simply a matter of time." He nodded and vanished from the chamber.

As a Wayfarer employed by the League, you will discover a measure of freedom you never thought possible. To be sure, you will have assignments and duties and much to be accomplished. However, when you have completed your missions, there will come occasion when all manner of experience is within your reach. When such occurs, you will find yourself unencumbered by time or circumstance or any lack whatsoever. All of history becomes open to you. For a time, you may find this experience one of wonderment and awe but such thoughts are bound to fade in the Eternal that is NOW.

When you were part of the Collective Illusion, so much of life was bounded by destination and achievement – one goal leading to another as you pursued what you hoped to become. Such is not the case in the Eternal. When time is not a parameter, each moment is part of a never-ending process. No longer are you involved in becoming; instead, your existence is simply to be.

Excerpt, "Introduction Orientation," *A Time Traveler's Code of Conduct* **by Ruth #7**

EIGHT: *Journal Entry – November 27 ATL*

According to the reckoning of the ATL, today is November 27. It is a fact I find most difficult to contemplate as it means our commencement is but nine days hence. Since my arrival, I have often found myself longing for the end of classes and homework. It is therefore somewhat surprising to feel restlessness in considering the unfoldment of what comes next. To be sure, the activities of a Wayfarer appear to contain some measure of freedom. Nevertheless, I am ever more cognizant of my present circumstance in which my independence has become subservient to both the League and my personal attachments, which are never far from mind.

Glancing back at these pages before me, I find that I failed to record what transpired after my encounter with Emmett. I should note that upon my return I journeyed immediately to the administrative offices and shared my encounter with the Governor-General, Milton #71, and Ruth #7. Although Sara and Milton seemed startled by Emmett's statement, "I have a number of ways to determine what you and other members of the League have been doing," Ruth was not. Whether it was an idea that had never occurred to the two before or whether the statement suggested that someone might be providing assistance, my telling of it prompted much concern. Ruth reminded us that her previous experience with Emmett suggested he would do anything in pursuit of his alternate timeline. After several additional questions from the three, I excused myself so that I might attend to my regular schedule. What did become clear during our discussion, however, is that the League remains focused on finding the best course of action to pursue Emmett and put an end to his efforts.

The day after my return, Agnes specifically set aside class time in the agenda for oral presentations of the remaining two ATL Mission Office assignments. I volunteered to go ahead of Bonne Soeur Marie, but as I have already provided a quick summation of my overall experience in Africa concerning both Emmett and the Manden Charter, I choose to note only two things about my report. The first is that I failed to mention my Emmett encounter to either Agnes or the class. (However, I was quick to discuss the experience with both my roomie and my sweetheart shortly thereafter.)

The second is that during my presentation I made liberal use of Agnes's stylus, writing as many words on the board as possible for personal emphasis: "Sundiata Keita," "Islam," "Gold," "Rice," "Salt," and the like, all of which prompted Agnes to comment, "Ben, that was exceedingly well-done!" at the conclusion of my oration. When I had finished, Bonne Soeur Marie moved to the front of the classroom and erased all of the words I had inscribed upon the board. In their place, she wrote only one name before us, "Paracelsus," and proceeded with her report.

She began with, "A man who was both challenging and talented . . . Un homme très compliqué—a very complicated man."

She then described how Paracelsus first learned the fundamentals of the sciences from his own father: medicine, botany, philosophy, and even mining. As he grew older, he continued to study medicine and the early science of alchemy, as he was drawn to both. He earned a degree in medicine and soon practiced as both a physician and a professor. He possessed a brilliant mind and gained an understanding of science and healing that surpassed most of his contemporaries.

"These are things for which he demonstrated talent," she assured us, "but his personality proved to be quite difficult . . . so difficult that he often found himself evicted from one town after another, becoming a wanderer for much of his early life."

According to Soeur Marie, he was prone to insulting those he believed to be less educated than himself. He once told a crowd, "Every little hair on my neck is far wiser than each of you and your scribes." He publicly burned the books of physicians and philosophers he thought were incorrect, untested, or inane. He was also very much disposed to the personal excesses of gluttony and drink.

After extensive travels throughout Europe, it was the harshness of his personality that threatened to have him evicted from Switzerland, the country of his birth. Soeur Marie's time travel mission was to rectify the situation as it was in opposition to the ATL and the dissemination of his ideas that would occur after his death. In fact, during the Renaissance, Paracelsus's understanding of science and healing was destined to transform much of medical understanding. Truly, he was a man ahead of his time.

Paracelsus demanded that wounds were to be cleaned as a means of preventing infection. He encouraged physicians to observe symptoms in order to discover the underlying disease. He was among the first to use chemicals and minerals as pharmacopeia in medicine. He invented liniment as a soothing ointment and introduced the concept of diagnostic medicine. He created a medical volume describing common illnesses and their appropriate treatment. He was the first to suggest that one's state of mind had an impact upon health. He even championed the humane treatment of the mentally ill, saying they were not possessed by evil spirits (as was often surmised) but instead were afflicted with a treatable illness.

Just as Bonne Soeur Marie had completed her report, summarizing how her influence had maintained the approved timeline, the school's emergency buzzer began ringing throughout the facility. The overwhelming sound brought all discussion to a halt. Soeur Marie stepped aside as Agnes moved impatiently to the front of the classroom. It was evident that our instructress was anxious as she looked repeatedly toward the doorway for signs of the mission's arrival. Each of my fellow classmates alternately glanced amongst us or looked toward either our teacher or the door. There was little else to be done in such a situation. The blaring sound of the alarm continued; we waited.

While the buzzer continued to ring out, Louise #217 finally arrived at the classroom. Agnes hurriedly took the pages from her hand and began reading. Louise glanced once in my direction, winked, and turned to depart. While the emergency sound continued, Agnes examined the ATL Mission Overview, bobbing about as she read it to herself. The alarm finally came to an end just as she turned her eyes from the document.

"We have an emergency assignment, vying for prominence with the approved timeline!" she waved her stylus toward Bonne Soeur Marie. "This one is for you. Pay close attention!"

Agnes turned to the board, writing four words as she said them aloud, "White Rock, British Columbia." She added nervously, "We have a vector-borne zoonotic disease to deal with!"

"What?" my roomie asked aloud, just as Agnes wrote, "Vector" and "Zoonotic" on the board with appropriate underlines.

"That means a disease that came from animals . . . this one was transmitted by a mosquito."

Bonne Soeur Marie was quick to inquire, "Quel est le problème? What is the problem?"

Agnes jumped about nervously, "In 2293, a teenage girl will be bitten by a mosquito. It leaves her unable to bear a child . . . this cannot occur. Her child must be born!"

"Who is the child?" George inquired.

"That is not of ultimate importance," Agnes replied quickly. "It is the birth of the child's child, the granddaughter, which must take place. Her name will be Olivia Clarke."

Emanuel was first to inquire, "Who is this Olivia Clarke?"

Agnes was forthright, "She is to become President of North America."

Shortly after Bonne Soeur Marie's #304 departure, the Governor-General called a special meeting within the massive chamber of the Akasha Library. On this occasion, I was able to take a seat near the front with Athena sitting next to me on one side and my roomie on the other.

Governor-General Sara #11 and Elder Professor Grimwald #94 stood in front of more than twenty-some chairs that had been hastily arranged for the occasion. Grimwald held several pieces of paper in his hand, which he and Sara appeared to be discussing. I looked around at those gathered and noticed that Milton #71 had taken a seat on the other end of the front row. Agnes found a place near the back, next to Nashwa #86. Everyone within the facility hurried to find a seat, including my remaining classmates. When most of the chairs had filled, the Governor-General provided a few introductory remarks before turning to Grimwald, asking him to explain the purpose of our gathering.

All at once, I felt a woman's hand on each of my shoulders. The scent of French perfume came to my nostrils as her hands proceeded to massage my shoulders. I turned to see Louise and shook my head in the negative. Athena spun her own head around and stared angrily just as Louise removed her hands and whispered, "Hello, my dear friends."

Elder Professor Grimwald continued speaking, ". . . and

so, I have been giving a great deal of thought to this matter of Emmett's alternate timeline . . ."

"He needs to be eradicated," Agnes interrupted from the back of the room.

"To be sure," Grimwald continued, "Emmett hopes to create a timeline that will displace our own. Clearly for him to do so would require a very stable timeline. After pondering the situation for many, many hours, I finally came to a conclusion that should have been most obvious to each of us this entire time."

Grimwald stopped speaking and looked out at the faces before him. He seemed in no hurry to relate his thoughts, as he simply continued to observe the audience. For some measure of time, there was only silence. Finally, Emma #119 spoke; she was clearly irritated. "Professor Grimwald, just tell us what you are thinking!" She shook her head in frustration and then pushed her horned-rimmed spectacles back up the bridge of her nose. "What should have been obvious to us this entire time?"

Elder Professor Grimwald nodded before continuing, "As we all know, Emmett needs to be working with a timeline in close alignment with the ATL. For that reason, it is most certain that this timeline could never have been in opposition to our own."

The old man stopped speaking, gazing upon the audience as though he was looking for anyone among us to understand the implications. Aside from Milton and Sara who were already obviously informed of the situation, no one seemed to be aware of what he was suggesting. The silence continued. Emma shook her head in disgust but said nothing. When it became clear that no one was cognizant of his implication, he finally resumed.

"Since Emmett's rival timeline would never have

been in opposition to our own, it stands to reason that no Time Traveler would have ever been sent on a mission to that location. This thought prompted me to wonder if we could discover—since the very beginning of the League—how many existing timelines within the records of the Akasha had never been assigned a mission. I was able to obtain just such an answer from the ATL Mission Office."

Before Grimwald could speak further, Emma asked impatiently, "What is the number?"

"There are 2,857 possible timelines that fit this description," came his response. He held up the pages in his hand and added, "I have had them all listed here in numerical order."

"What!" George stated aloud. "That seems like a lot!"

Grimwald was undeterred, "Perhaps, but it is far fewer than the infinite possibilities we had been considering previously. Certainly, 2,857 is not infinite . . . I am suggesting that we begin with the first timeline on the list—timeline XLIX."

Although a few whispered some thought or another amongst themselves, most remained silent. Finally, it was Milton #71 who rose to address those gathered. "Thank you, Elder Professor Grimwald. This is extremely helpful." He turned to assure us, "This should be good news to us all. Although it may take time to adequately deal with this situation, 2,857 is certainly a workable number. At last, we know where to begin."

George turned to me and said, "It still seems like a lot."

Within a day of Elder Professor Grimwald's revelation, we were informed by Agnes #23 that the ATL Mission office had requested "all hands on deck" (this was the exact phrase used by our instructress) and that each of us would receive a timeline assignment shortly. The League was going to place some of its focus on finding Emmett's whereabouts, putting an end to his endeavors. From Agnes's description, it was apparent that both Wayfarers and students alike were to be assigned an independent mission to one of Grimwald's 2,857 timelines. Although the wisdom of sending us on these assignments alone rather than in pairs had apparently been debated among the Core, the deciding factor was simply that we could accomplish the task twice as fast with one Time Traveler than could be done with two.

Upon learning of these new undertakings, we students could not help but be overwhelmed. These newest missions were to be in addition to our regular curriculum, homework, timeline assignments, and the inevitable studying necessary for the upcoming final. George seemed to speak for each of us with one simple statement, "You have got to be kidding!"

As Agnes announced the League's plan for these new assignments, Nashwa #86 sat quietly toward the front of our classroom. At first, I pondered whether Nashwa was there as a member of the Core or simply for our teacher's moral support. Both thoughts were quickly tossed aside, however, when Agnes informed us of her planned curriculum for the morning.

"You will be excited to learn that today we have a very special guest speaker!" Our teacher bobbed about as she wrote the name "Nashwa #86" on the board. "My good friend, Nashwa, is going to tell you about another one of her experiences as a Wayfarer on the front lines! Please, join me in welcoming her!"

Agnes began applauding enthusiastically (looking sternly at each of us until we did likewise) and smiled from one ear to the other as Nashwa rose from her seat and walked to the front of the classroom. Agnes ushered Nashwa to the proper place to stand before moving toward one of the empty student desks to take a seat.

Nashwa turned to us and began, "Over the years, I have had some amazing experiences as a Wayfarer, and many interesting missions along the way . . ."

Agnes interrupted, "And she has done them so well!"

"Thank you, Agnes," Nashwa replied, appearing only somewhat embarrassed by the outburst. "This morning, I want to tell you about one of them. Rather than getting into unnecessary details, let me just say that the assignment dealt with the Tetrarchy—a system of government put in place by the Roman Emperor Diocletian."

As soon as the word had been spoken, Bonne Soeur Marie lifted her hand high above her head, prompting Nashwa to add quickly, "A tetrarchy means four people trying to rule the empire together."

Agnes interrupted again, "You might want to write that word on the board!"

Nashwa nodded, complied with the request, and continued, "Diocletian created a ruling system in which there would be two emperors, who divided the empire between them, and two assistant emperors, responsible for helping the first two. Although he assumed such a system would give the empire greater organization and structure, it eventually caused a series of civil wars between the ruling factions. After Diocletian retired and several rulers had come and gone, the four in place were Maximinus, Severus, Licinius, and Constantine."

All at once, Agnes began bobbing about in her chair. The commotion caused Nashwa to stop speaking; she turned inquisitively to observe her friend. The look of confusion upon Nashwa's face suggested she was wondering what was causing our teacher's erratic movements. A moment later, Nashwa suddenly seemed to understand as she quickly turned to write the four names on the board: "Maximinus," "Severus," "Licinius," and "Constantine."

Agnes breathed a sigh of relief, and Nashwa continued. "Let me add that before Diocletian's retirement he had personally chosen Maximinus as his successor. For this reason, it was not long before Severus's armies chose to align with Maximinus, abandoning Severus in the process. Conflict soon arose between Constantine and Licinius, as well."

Our guest speaker gazed at the looks of confusion before her and simplified the matter immediately. "My assignment was to help unify the Roman Empire under Constantine—that is the approved timeline. In the face of such division, it was not easy. The conflict between these various groups lasted for nearly 20 years."

Nashwa shook her head in dismay as she recalled her multiple challenges, "Even when I managed to influence Licinius to align with Constantine over some issue or another, a problem occurred with Maximinus. On most timelines, Severus became the first of the four to die, putting much of his portion of the empire into disarray." She eyed us all closely, "Not everyone, however, was as eager to overthrow Severus as had been his army. Those that still followed him remained rebellious. I found myself facing one difficulty after another. Over and over again, I used my influence on one or more of the emperors and countless subordinates only to fail repeatedly." She smiled, "I am certain you

know the approach we need to follow when a Wayfarer
is confronted by failure?"

"Begin again!" several of us spoke in unison.

"Exactly. Begin again." Nashwa nodded in appreciation.
"As some of you have already experienced, when you face
a problem on these mission assignments it may be best to
change your perspective and discover new insight. It was
that very motivation that led me to Constantine's mother,
Helena. She was one of the early converts to Christianity."

Nashwa paused before interjecting, "Let me give you
some additional background information . . . "

The statement prompted Agnes to perk up in her chair.
I turned to look at George, who was smiling.

Our guest speaker continued, "Much of the Roman
Empire was in chaos by the time of Constantine's birth. The
empire had grown so large that it encompassed countless
citizens who possessed absolutely no allegiance to Rome.
By the Fourth Century, the empire had also become so
diverse that it consisted of individuals from all known
religions. Even for many who had been born in Rome, the
appeal of the pagan gods no longer served as a central part
of daily life. I decided to use this fact and the knowledge
I had discovered about Helena as a way of inspiring
Constantine."

Nashwa paused for a moment as she called to mind her
experience, "At the Battle of Milvian Bridge, just beyond
the outskirts of Rome, I influenced Constantine and his
generals to see an enormous cross in the clouds as the one
symbol that could unite them all . . . "

My Swede friend, Emanuel, was quick to interrupt,
"You caused him to see the cross of fire in the sky?"

Our guest speaker nodded, "Yes, and the dream he
had that very night. You know, quite a number of Time
Travelers have used dreams to influence their mission
targets . . ."

Emanuel interrupted again, "I always believed the experience was Divinely inspired!"

Nashwa was undeterred, "Even the Highest Authority has occasional need of a Time Traveler." She continued, "Constantine took it as a sign. He proved victorious in battle. During his reign, he promoted the acceptance of Christianity, established the eastern capital of Constantinople, and unified the eastern portion of the empire. His empire would remain in place for more than 1,000 years after his death. The mission was a success. I needed to begin again many, many times but, eventually, the mission was a success."

Before another word could be spoken, Agnes rose from her seat and began applauding enthusiastically. She looked upon us, making it entirely clear that we were to join in such approval. "Everyone, please join me in thanking Nashwa for her report."

Our teacher sighed with admiration, "Oh, Nashwa, you are such an inspiration!"

As I have repeatedly noted within this journal, the process of time travel to another period within the Collective Illusion involves the consciousness of falling. Although the experience is one I have personally encountered on many different occasions, it is not one undertaken with any measure of calm. I have yet to discern whether this unease is due to the fact that the traveler has no semblance of control over the process or because of the various unknowns regarding the mission one is soon to encounter. In either case, the fall involves some level of apprehension. Perhaps I will need to explore this matter further.

On this occasion, as the wind rushed past my extremities and I sensed the helplessness of having my body plunge to the ground below, I attempted to place my mind elsewhere by contemplating how long it might take the League to explore all 2,857 timelines listed within Grimwald's pages. All nine of us involved in Milton's original search for League deserters would be participating in these new assignments. Ruth #7 had even volunteered to visit timeline XLIX — the first on the list. In addition to these nine, I reasoned that we could perhaps recruit an additional seven or eight Wayfarers. (I cannot say with any certainty whether this number might be higher, as no one has yet informed me how many Wayfarers are a part of the League's activities.)

Taking into account the League's regular "business as usual," as Agnes often refers to such matters, and the fact that each of us has multiple duties and assignments that are already a part of our responsibilities, I assumed that all those involved might average two timeline excursions per month. I performed the necessary ciphering within my head and calculated that at such a pace we would be able to visit each of the timelines in question in approximately seven years. The result prompted me to agree with my roomie's original assessment, "It still seems like a lot."

When the fall finally came to its end, I found my vaporous form enveloping the body of Alexander. My ghostly self continuously swirled about in waves of motion that encircled the king as he turned to speak to one of the warriors reclining nearby. I gave thought to separating myself from my target, and a moment later found that I was standing next to the ruler, observing the banquet before me for the third time.

To be sure, what I perceived was quite similar to the celebration I had viewed previously. Everyone relaxed in some semblance of recline—eating and conversing amongst themselves as though dining on the floor was far preferable to sitting at a table and chair. Pillows and cushions remained scattered about with soldiers using such support to position themselves near the abundant foodstuffs placed nearby. As before, a number of those present wore leaves and flowers like a crown upon their heads, and the smells of perfume, cinnamon, bread, and poultry filled the air. Alexander, himself, continued to possess the appearance of a man of great strength. His abundant hair fell down upon a pronounced forehead and muscular shoulders. It was readily apparent that I stood in the presence of a man in the prime of his life.

What I perceived was very much the same as it had been on my two previous occasions. At the same time, however, there were differences. In addition to the presence of various attendants that I had not seen beforehand, and a more frequent use of the color blue in the attire of the warriors before me, I sensed that the mind of this king was far more balanced in thought. Although conquest remained a subject of his personal contemplation, of equal import was his love of reading, writing, and playing the lyre. This Alexander felt as equally drawn to quiet reclusion as he was to the sociable exchanges that are experienced in the presence of others. Whereas the king I had encountered during my previous visitations seemed more self-indulgent and impulsive, this Alexander appeared to hold himself to a higher standard and was more pensive than the one I had visited earlier.

While these thoughts entered my mind, I watched one of the attendants place a platter of gizzards and onions before the king. As before, Alexander smiled and took three of the morsels into his mouth and chewed them hungrily. It was in the midst of such observation that I heard Emmett's voice come from behind.

"Hello Ben," he said calmly.

I turned swiftly to see the ghostly forms of Emmett and Bruce #29 swirling before my eyes.

"What are you doing here?" were the words that came to me.

Emmett chuckled, shaking his white hair as he spoke, "I told you there are ways of knowing what the League is doing." He paused for a moment before adding, "I briefly considered an encounter with Ruth on timeline XLIX but I would much rather speak with you."

I could not help but be surprised, "You know where Ruth is?"

"Absolutely," he spoke with authority, "I also know of Grimwald's list and the 2,857 timelines the League plans to visit, and the fact that your first assignment was here on timeline CCCIV."

"Visiting 2,857 timelines is an enormous project!" Bruce said with disgust. "You would be better off coming with us."

Although I was certain of the answer beforehand, I replied nonetheless, "So this is not the alternate timeline of your creation?"

Bruce shook his head in the negative just as Emmett replied, "No, this is but a lesser timeline with no impact upon either the ATL or the timeline where we focus our endeavors."

I inquired, "Who is the 'we' that remains involved in such a project?"

Emmett laughed before responding, "That is something you will know only when you choose to join us."

As soon as Emmett had spoken, Alexander's senior general, Perdiccas, entered the room and lowered himself to his place on the floor. Like those around him, the general remained completely oblivious to the three vaporous forms standing and conversing in the midst of the banquet.

"What are you doing here?" I repeated my earlier query.

Emmett nodded, "I want to show you something."

He paused, and so I inquired, "What is it?"

Rather than uttering another word, Emmett bent down to whisper in Bruce's ear. The shorter man listened intently, nodding twice as the old Keeper of the Records spoke. Although I could hear whispers, the only word I clearly understood was "Olympias." A moment after the old man had finished his instructions, the ghostly form of Bruce disappeared from the room.

After Bruce was gone, I inquired, "Why did you mention Olympias?"

"As you are no doubt aware, she is the mother of Alexander."

I inquired further, "Where is Bruce?"

"He has gone to alter the timeline."

"What do you mean?" I felt a measure of surprise and worry.

"Olympias is a devotee of Dionysus . . . are you familiar with the name?" Emmett eyed me closely.

"Is that not the god of harvest, wine, and fertility?" I recalled from my youthful studies.

"Very good," came Emmett's reply, "What you may not know is that there were devotees of Dionysus who chose to profess their faith by the practice of sleeping with snakes."

My eyes opened wide in alarm.

Emmett shook his hand from side to side and continued, "Obviously, snakes chosen for such devotion were harmless in nature. Olympias numbers herself among those involved in such dedication to her god."

I pondered his words for but a moment before confessing, "I do not understand."

He spoke without emotion, "Bruce has traveled to the year before Olympias becomes wedded to Phillip and gives birth to Alexander."

"For what purpose?"

He was straightforward, "He will influence a servant to place a more potent snake within her bedding."

"But you cannot influence someone against their will!"

Emmett chuckled again, "Do you really believe that all who serve Olympias remain devoted to her?" He pointed toward Alexander reclining upon the ground saying only, "Watch what comes next."

I turned to look at the king, simply observing him as he reached toward the platter for one morsel after another. The young man was jovial, his light reddish-brown curls bounced upon his head as he turned to speak to the warrior closest to him. Suddenly, there was a flash of light, and everything within the room changed before me.

Alexander was gone, and in his place sat an older, dark-haired man. He looked to be past the prime of middle age and possessed a thin battle scar upon one cheek. Rather than reclining like the Greeks who had been present but a moment earlier, he sat upright with his legs crossed in front of him. Each of the others within the room sat likewise, placing themselves in circular groups upon colorful carpets around copper trays filled with foodstuffs. Most of those present were completely attired in red. Each man held a knife in one hand as though it was a necessary appendage for such a banquet. Upon the trays, I could see eggplant, spinach, and beans. Meat with the smell of lamb or goat came into my nostrils. The room's colors had changed as well, giving way to blue and green and turquoise and red, with enormous carpets of similar hues hanging throughout the room's walls.

I pointed to the dark-haired man with the scar, sitting in our midst, "Who is he?" I wondered aloud.

"He is Darius III," Emmett replied. "He is the king of Persia."

"What of Alexander?"

"There is no such individual upon this timeline. He was never born," Emmett replied simply. "Olympias died before she was ever wedded. As a result, she was never able to undermine Phillip. As such, Phillip remains very much alive. He is the ruler of Macedonia, although it is a smaller kingdom than the one overseen by a son who is no more."

"You changed the timeline!"

Emmett smiled, "Changing a timeline is not difficult in the least. Causing a timeline to take precedence over the ATL, however, proves to be much more challenging. Do not worry yourself, this is a lesser timeline. Its multiple changes will have no impact upon the ATL."

His words prompted me to inquire, "What multiple changes?"

"There are many," the old man assured me. "When Alexander died on the approved timeline, Greece became separated into rival fractions. On this timeline, however, Phillip's kingdom remains united. In this rendition of history, there will be no city of Alexandria and there will be no Great Library. Since Alexander did not conquer Persia, the Persian Empire continues and Darius remains its ruler. In fact, the kingdoms of Persia, Greece, and Rome will persist for a very long time to come . . . the list of changes goes on."

"Why?" I could not help but ask.

Emmett shrugged, "To demonstrate how such things

are of very little import. For the League to remain focused on keeping the ATL in alignment with some grandeur plan is nothing but foolishness. It is a never-ending waste of senseless hope and everlasting labor. Surely, a man of your intellect has seen this already?"

I was defiant, "I will not join you!"

Emmett only nodded, "Very well. You and the League can continue in this folly. I anticipate that others who have had a change of mind will follow me shortly. When you have grown tired of engaging in these meaningless pursuits, let me know."

Without speaking another word, the old man vanished from my sight.

Since the inception of Moment One, and the League's coming into existence shortly thereafter, our principal goal has been nothing less than the Prime Directive. In spite of this mandate, it is but a common occurrence for Wayfarers within this profession — so focused on timelines and the rectification of countless events throughout the Collective Illusion — to temporarily lose sight of the goal. For that reason, it may be helpful to bring to mind the very reason for your own recruitment and induction.

You were called to this work for a reason, just as those before you. Something about your life brought you to the attention of the Core. To be sure, even now that something may be necessary for maintaining the sanctity of a timeline but it means so much more. Your individual missions along the way are simply part of a process leading to a much grander goal — a goal within the illusion of space-time that will, ultimately, transform all of consciousness. Only you can come to understand how your involvement is instrumental in bringing the Prime Directive into manifestation at last.

Excerpt, "The Prime Directive," *A Time Traveler's Code of Conduct* **by Ruth #7**

NINE: *Journal Entry — December 2 ATL*

I had an obligation to report to members of the Core my most recent encounter with Emmett, and the timeline alteration I had witnessed firsthand. As soon as I returned, I made my way to the administrative wing of the League facility. I walked quickly past the door of the ATL Mission Office (as a means of avoiding Louise) and journeyed straight to the office of the Governor-

General. Upon my arrival, I waited for Sara #11 to summon Milton #71 and Ruth #7. It was not long before we four had assembled in Meeting Room 2. I chose to sit next to Sara. Ruth and Milton each took a seat on the other side of the table.

As soon as we had taken our places, Milton provided a quick assessment of his latest observations of the shadowy timeline he had been watching. He discussed how its appearance continued to materialize, only to disappear shortly thereafter. His conclusion was unmistakable, "It continues to grow in strength. Although it remains ephemeral, it continues to grow in strength."

Sara sighed but added, "As long as it remains as a shadow, we have time." She then turned to me, "Ben, tell us what you saw."

I began my tale with a brief description of the fall I had experienced journeying to timeline CCCIV. I explained that during the process (all too familiar to each of those present), I had decided to calculate how long it might take to explore all 2,857 timelines contained within Elder Professor Grimwald's listing. I explained how I had arrived at the figure of "approximately seven years," but quickly added, "The calculation was made with the assumption that the League might engage perhaps 16 or 17 Time Travelers for an extended period in just such an undertaking. Obviously, as I do not know how many Wayfarers currently find themselves under the League's supervision, the calculation might be very much flawed."

Although I looked about the room for some semblance of clue as to the accuracy of my estimation, there was none. Instead, Milton conjectured aloud, "I do not believe we will have seven years before Emmett's timeline gains prominence over our own."

I continued the tale, including my own assessment that the Alexander on this timeline seemed more balanced in thought than the one I had previously encountered within the ATL. I went on to describe how Emmett and Bruce #29 had appeared shortly thereafter. I was also quick to include, "Emmett made it extremely clear that he not only knew my whereabouts, but he knew that Ruth had journeyed to timeline XLIX."

Milton was concerned, "That is most alarming."

"Someone is definitely helping him," Sara concluded, adding, "Someone within the League facility is communicating with him."

Suddenly recalling what Athena had told me earlier, I inquired, "Do you think someone is sending messages to his Horologium?"

Sara, Milton, and Ruth looked at each other. It was Ruth who responded, "That is extremely likely."

Sara motioned for me to continue.

I described how during my encounter with our old Keeper of the Records and Bruce, both tried to convince me that the work of the League was simply a waste of time. I explained how I had wondered aloud whether timeline CCCIV was Emmett's alternate timeline, only to have him respond, ". . . this is but a lesser timeline with no impact upon either the ATL or the timeline where we are focusing our endeavors . . ."

Ruth interrupted, "Emmett may not be entirely accurate in that assessment."

I was quick to inquire, "What do you mean?"

She explained, "Ben, the influence of a timeline and its weakness or supremacy is completely interwoven with the activities and interactions of every individual upon that timeline. As soon as you create change for those most directly involved, the vibration of the timeline can be altered. A change of this magnitude could have serious consequences for what was once a lesser timeline."

Milton added, "Olympias was a major figure in her time. She was personally responsible for the demise of those that got in her way, and many of her rivals. In her absence, numerous shifts in history might become possible."

"But the ATL system will alert us if the timeline vies for prominence," Sara reassured me. "Ben, please continue."

I went on to describe the disappearance of Bruce #29 — how he had journeyed to the past, and how Alexander had been replaced by the subsequent appearance of Darius III shortly thereafter. I then recalled how Emmett had smiled and spoken the words, "Changing a timeline is not difficult in the least. Causing a timeline to take precedence over the ATL, however, proves to be much more challenging."

Before anyone could respond further, I suddenly recalled something Bruce had spoken aloud to Emmett on the occasion when I had first observed the two. "I just remembered something!" I said excitedly.

The three turned to me and waited.

I described what I recalled. "Sara, when you gave me your Horologium and I went back and encountered Emmett and Bruce without their knowledge, Bruce said something that seemed most unusual at the time. I do not know what it means, but I am certain it means something."

Ruth was intrigued, "What did he say?"

I nodded. "Bruce said that, because of the approach Emmett had chosen to create his duplicate ATL, 'there is much more that needs to be done.'"

For a few moments, there was only silence. Finally, it was the Governor-General who inquired of the group, "What do you think it means?"

"I do not know," came Milton's reply.

Ruth reflected upon the statement a while longer and then surmised, "He is doing something more involved than changing one timeline. Obviously, it is something designed to make our efforts to stop him even more challenging."

In spite of our collective exhaustion and the pressure of the final that weighed heavily upon the class, the next morning we students had gathered in the League Café during the morning break for some semblance of respite, sustenance, and conversation. I had already eaten my usual fare (consisting of a muffin with honey) and was pleasantly engaged sipping coffee from my mug. In a similar manner, each of my classmates had devoured whatever provision they found most appealing. We had assembled ourselves at one of the larger tables in the center of the room. Although the research demands of these new assignments prevented Athena from joining us, out of habit my classmates had left available one of the chairs next to me.

While we were eating, Bonne Soeur Marie provided additional details on her timeline mission to the year 2293, and her rectification of the vector-borne zoonotic disease that nearly prevented the birth of one Olivia Clark more than thirty-five years later. "Très intéressant . . . it was very interesting. I moved forward in time and watched Canada and the States join to form one united country. British Columbia was the first to suggest such a union." She added, "Quebec was the last."

I expressed my own astonishment, "That is quite a surprise. During my time, it was French-speaking Quebec that nearly joined the colonists in opposition to British rule."

We sat quietly in seeming contemplation of such a merger until Emanuel finally inquired, "Is everyone ready for the final? It seems like it is here much too soon."

Manuela #64 waved her spoon in his direction, "Do you not remember, time is nothing more than an illusion." She smiled, placing her spoon upon the table and then taking a drink from her cup.

Bonne Soeur Marie pondered aloud, "Much remains to be studied."

My roomie added his own thoughts on the situation, "We have certainly covered a lot of material . . . I hope Agnes doesn't expect us to remember all of it."

Emanuel replied, "For any multiple-choice question, I propose the process of elimination. Generally, using this approach, one can narrow the answers down to one or two. In terms of the essay portion, I recommend the liberal use of names, double underlines, and as much background information as you can recall. These are the things that Agnes #23 finds most appealing."

George confessed, "I think I need more time to study."

Manuela #64 took another sip from her cup and turned the conversation toward our latest mission assignments, "I found my journey to the Alexander timeline most interesting!" She glanced at me and added, "It was my first encounter with the king, so I do not know if it was similar to your experience, but I found him to be most reluctant in the role that fate had thrust upon him. He was more drawn to reading, the arts, and to his music than he was to the battlefield." She quickly added, "Emmett was not there."

Bonne Soeur Marie shook her head in disagreement, "Pour moi . . . for me, I found Alexander to be most comfortable as a soldier and a leader of other men. He was much the same when Ben and I first journeyed to the banquet." She turned to me, looking for concurrence. It was a moment before I could swallow my coffee and agree, "Truly he was just such a man on our first encounter but he seemed much more balanced in thought on this occasion . . ."

Emanuel interrupted, "It is but proof of the words in our text! Remember?" He looked at each of us in turn. "In Ruth's chapter about revisiting timelines, we learned that the very same individual might make different choices upon different timelines."

My roomie shook his head in frustration, "I hope Agnes isn't going to ask which chapter contains which concept!"

"Truly, we will know soon enough," Emanuel was quick to reply.

"I would not worry about it," I reassured him. "Such a level of detail is surely beyond the needs of any Time Traveler."

George seemed relieved, while Emanuel added, "Time and again, I have been impressed with Ruth's wisdom. Among members of the Core, she appears to be most learned of all."

I volunteered, "She certainly understands all matters of our work, the League, and even how Emmett thinks." I glanced quickly at my roomie but said no more.

Manuela continued her personal observations, "I believe the Alexander on my mission assignment would have been better suited as the son of a writer or a musician. Those were the things he longed to pursue."

Soeur Marie disagreed, "My Alexander wanted conquest."

George added his own assessment, "My own mission found a king very much focused on matters of the heart. Truly, he seemed to have a special affection for a young Persian named Bagoas . . ."

A French voice interrupted from behind me, "We are all drawn to such matters of the heart! Are we not?"

I was quick to reply, "Hello, Louise." Without another word, she took the seat next to me. I turned nervously toward my roomie, looking for help in the matter.

George understood the situation immediately, as he reminded my fellow students, "We need to get back to class. Agnes is waiting for us."

Emanuel and Bonne Soeur Marie were the first to rise from the table. I tried to do likewise but as George stood and took his tray, Louise placed her hand upon my arm and told the others, "I need to speak with Ben for only a moment . . . He will be along shortly."

My roomie looked at me helplessly before turning and leaving the table with Manuela.

When Louise and I were very much alone, she smiled. She took my arm and whispered ever-so-softly, "I have decided we must pursue a compromise in this situation we find ourselves in."

I was confused, "A compromise? What situation?"

Louise smiled, "Oh my darling, obviously, we cannot ignore this connection between us . . . Can we?" Her blue eyes stared at me intensely; she sighed.

I stammered, "I am not sure what you are saying?"

Her words were to the point, "We need to allow ourselves to satisfy this longing we both feel, and yet we must be considerate of Athena and her feelings . . . do we not? I know that you find me beautiful. Is that not so?"

I stammered, "Athena is my sweetheart, Louise. That is not going to change."

"Nor should it," she agreed. "It is for this very reason

that I have found a solution to this problem among the three of us."

I could only say, "I do not understand."

She smiled. "Tell Athena that in such a situation I find myself most agreeable to an idea that will enable us all to get what we need." She added quickly, "In the twenty-first century they have called such an understanding a 'throuple.' I am most certain you would find such an arrangement most acceptable."

I was very much confused, "I believe I am unfamiliar with the term."

Louise leaned closer, placed a kiss on the side of my mouth, and added, "Just tell your Athena that I am most agreeable to the idea."

Without speaking another word, she stood from the table, turned, and headed out the doorway in the direction of the League's administrative offices.

"Liverpool!" Agnes said excitedly, as she underlined the word on the board before us. "Liverpool," she repeated, "is one of those places that has frequently demonstrated the illusory nature of time. If only those individuals who are trapped within the Collective Illusion would simply choose to look!"

(I should note herein that after class I told my roomie that I had once made a visit to Liverpool in 1759, with my son William. Imagine my surprise when George informed me that Liverpool had been the very location of the first branch of his business in England due to its port.)

Agnes shook her head in disgust and proceeded
to walk back and forth in front of the class, gripping
the ever-present stylus in hand. She appeared deep in
thought as she traversed the length of her desk and
back, making the journey three times in succession
before turning to wave the stylus at each of us in turn,
exclaiming, "In Liverpool, you can hear one amazing
story after another!"

"Do you perhaps have some background information
you could share with us?" George inquired, attempting
to appear quite serious in the matter.

Our instructress turned toward him and slapped the
top of her desk, "Portions of this will be on your final
exam . . ." She reminded us, "And the exam is only two
days away!"

She collected her thoughts, "Now where was I? Oh
yes . . . by this time in your education, you won't be
surprised to learn that there are locations within the
Collective Illusion where time slips are more prevalent
than others." She nodded in the affirmative. "Liverpool,
England is one such place."

Her pacing resumed as she volunteered, "Some say
that Liverpool's many time slips are due to the presence
of ley lines."

Bonne Soeur Marie's hand shot straight up in the air
as she interrupted, "Madame Agnes, I am not familiar
with these ley lines."

Our teacher brushed aside the interruption with a
wave of her hand and continued, "Ley lines are energy
threads around the earth that somehow align with the
placement of ancient sites. There are those who believe
that Liverpool's underground subway system crossed
these lines. Others say that the residue of so much
unresolved conflict from the very people who once
lived in Liverpool created an unstable time vortex. No

one knows for certain, but whatever the reason, there is something quite unusual about the place!"

She went on to inform us that the Liverpool settlement was originally founded by King John in 1207. At the time, it was nothing more than a tiny village, but as it possessed a riverway with access to the Irish Sea and the Atlantic Ocean, five hundred years later it would grow to become a massive shipping port with an abundance of trade.

"Including the slave trade!" our teacher added, shaking her head in disgust. "It became a major city, attracting Irish and Scottish immigrants looking for work. Because it brought together so many settlers in search of a better life, it had more than its share of impoverished and destitute. During World War II, the port and much of the city were bombed by the Nazis. After that, and for much of the twentieth century, Liverpool found itself in decline."

"Those are the basics!" She slapped the top of her desk for emphasis, and then waved the stylus in front of her, "As I said, there have been quite a number of time slips in Liverpool! Let me tell you my favorite."

Agnes turned and wrote the words "Cripp's" and "Caplan's" on the board, each with a double underline.

"In July 1996, an Englishman named Frank and his wife Carol went shopping one morning in Liverpool. It was a beautiful day in the early spring—quite unusual for England at that time of year. After spending a couple of hours together, they decided to each visit one more store on their own before getting some lunch. Carol headed for Dillon's Bookshop and Frank wanted to go to the HMV music store to look at CDs. The plan was for Frank to come to Dillon's and find Carol as soon as he had finished."

She had a difficult time controlling her excitement.

"Now listen to what happens next! Surely, you recall
the Medieval time slip? Remember, the naval cadets
described the town and told their commanding officer,
'Something was very strange. We heard no sounds . . .
there was no wind.' That very same sensation came to
Frank as he left the music store and headed back down
the street to find Carol. Years later, when he told the
story to others, he said it was like 'walking through a
dead spot of quietness.'"

As a means of providing us with some measure of
a theatrical component to the tale, Agnes proceeded
to demonstrate large stepping motions with her feet,
describing what followed, "All at once, Frank felt
something unusual under his shoes." She looked down
to peer at her own feet. "The road was cobblestone!
Only a moment before it had been asphalt!" Our teacher
looked up and added for further clarification, "The
British call it tarmac."

She then began to look around the classroom. "Frank
was surprised to see that everyone was wearing clothes
from the 1950s! Most of the men wore overcoats and
hats; the women were dressed in full skirts, wearing
headscarves and gloves. The change of scenery was so
shocking that he came to a complete stop in the middle
of the street, prompting a van with the name 'Caplan's'
written on either side to honk its old horn as it sped past.
After being startled by both the sound and everything
around him, Frank hurried toward Dillon's Bookshop.
However, when he stood before the store where he
had left Carol not 30 minutes before, instead of books
he saw ladies' shoes and handbags on display in the
shop window. He looked up at the sign, but rather than
reading 'Dillon's Bookshop,' it read 'Cripp's.' Frank
was completely baffled. Then he suddenly realized that
he was not alone."

Agnes continued, "A woman stood next to him, appearing just as confused as Frank. When he turned to her, he realized that, like him, she was wearing clothes from the 1990s. She looked at him and spoke, 'I thought this was Dillon's?' Frank expressed his own confusion. Neither knew what they should do. Finally, having no other choice, the woman walked into the store; Frank followed after her."

Agnes spun around, "All at once there was a flash and the two found themselves back inside Dillon's Bookshop. They had returned to 1996! Frank grabbed the woman by the arm and asked, 'Did you see that?' She said she had."

Our teacher bobbed about excitedly. "Frank and the woman soon found Frank's wife. He told Carol what he had just seen, and the woman confirmed her own experience. Carol told them both that nothing unusual had occurred for her but Frank was adamant — somehow he had journeyed back through time to the 1950s."

Manuela #64 posed a query, "Did Frank ever look into either Caplan's or Cripp's?"

"He did!" Agnes replied excitedly. "Frank was a police officer, with quite a background in investigations. He decided to research the matter for himself. What he found was that Cripp's clothing store had been in that very location before Dillon's Bookshop, but it had closed in the 1970s; Caplan's was short for Louis Caplan's Sweet Shops, which had gone out of business even earlier."

Agnes spoke with certainty, "That is the Cripp's and Caplan's Time Slip!"

Once our instructress had finished her tale, my roomie posed a query. "Has anyone in these time slip experiences from the past ever made note of the fact that they saw someone from the future?"

Our teacher seemed confused, "I don't understand."

George continued, "In all of these stories, we have people from their own time describing how they encountered people from the past. For example, in the Moberly-Jourdain time slip, we heard how two women from the twentieth century were able to perceive Marie Antoinette and her entourage from more than a hundred years before. Is there any record that people from Marie Antoinette's time described seeing two women from the future?"

Agnes appeared uninterested, "Why does that matter?"

"It is just a question. I am trying to decide whether those in a time slip are seeing shadows of the past or have they actually traveled to the time and place where they perceive themselves to be?"

"Assuming you are serious," our instructress peered at him closely, "we know that these people from the past are able to see individuals from a time other than their own. Remember, the Caplan's' truck honked its horn at Frank. In Moberly-Jourdain, a beggar gave the two women directions. It is much more than perceiving shadows from the past. What they see is very, very real."

I whispered only to myself, "As real as the illusion of time can be."

"Aren't you worried at all about tomorrow's final exam?" My roomie inquired, looking up from the text, *A Time Traveler's Code of Conduct*, he had been reading.

I turned from the note pages I had been reviewing myself and glanced at him across our small tabletop. We had chosen the occasion for some quiet study within the confines of our own chambers. The look on George's face was one of great concern. I tried to reassure him, "I do not believe I would choose to use the word 'worry,' as it suggests having to deal with an experience over which one has little influence or control. That is not the case with an examination such as this. We have been present for every portion of the curriculum, and we have the ability to study, review, and prepare ourselves for what is to come."

George was unmoved, "You are not worried in the least?"

I gathered my thoughts. "It is inevitable that every student may feel some level of apprehension regarding the multiple unknowns of an exam such as this. To be sure, I am a student. Therefore, it seems most appropriate that I should feel some level of apprehension regarding Agnes's final."

My roomie managed a smile, "I do not believe that syllogism is to be a part of the examination."

I tried to encourage him, "Still, I would recommend refraining from worry as much as possible. You will do just fine on the exam."

"What do you think Agnes is going to ask us?"

I leaned forward to remind him, "She has already revealed to us several of her questions."

My roomie was quick to respond, "Really? Please remind me."

I counted them off on my fingertips. "We have the question about Hattie Jennings and the outcome had she gone into that house from the past. We have been advised that we need to possess some familiarity with each of the time slip accounts that were detailed

during our class time. We know that there will be some
semblance of questioning regarding major concepts she
has covered, such as the restraints that empower the
illusion of time." I reminded him, "Remember, time
zones are one such restraint. We can also be certain that
she will ask something about the scientific nature of
time and this business of gravity and motion."

"Anything else?" George wondered aloud.

"As we have frequently taken class time to review
these personal mission reports, I would wager she
will ask us to describe something about a Time
Travel assignment undertaken by someone other than
ourselves."

My roomie nodded in agreement, "You are probably
right." He turned back to the classroom text but soon
glanced in my direction as a thought came to him. "How
is Athena? I have not seen her for several days."

I replied, "She finds herself very much involved in
research for these newest mission assignments."

George was swift to inquire, "She's not mad about
the Louise situation, is she?"

"That is difficult to discern," came my honest reply.
"She is definitely not happy that Louise continues to
express an interest in me. As to whether she remains
mad at me because of Louise's behavior, I am uncertain."

"What did Louise want to talk about yesterday
morning?" He appeared very interested in my reply.

I pondered an appropriate response and then
managed to say, "I think I know what she wants but it
is not something that my sweetheart will want to hear."

My roomie was most intrigued, "What is it?"

I sighed, "Louise wants me to tell Athena that she
is most agreeable to an arrangement called a throuple."

George appeared confused, "A what?"

My words were straightforward, "I believe she is

suggesting an amorous relationship between the three of us."

At first, he seemed puzzled, "What?" But added shortly thereafter, "You mean a ménage à trois?"

I nodded. "I believe that is what she has in mind."

George could not help but chuckle, "Athena is going to kill you."

The hour of our final exam had arrived at last. The five of us sat in our usual classroom seats, repeatedly looking toward the doorway for any sign of our instructress. To be sure, Agnes was not late; instead, the apprehension of the undertaking had prompted the rest of us to arrive early.

George broke the silence, "I wish we could just get started."

"You will have the opportunity shortly," Emanuel replied, although his eyes remained fixated on the door.

"Should one of us go look for her?" Manuela pondered aloud.

I was in the midst of formulating a response when our teacher poked her head in the doorway. She did not enter the room. Instead, she placed only her head where we could see it and spoke with excitement, "I have a surprise for all of you!"

Bonne Soeur Marie was first to inquire, "Qu'est-ce que c'est . . . What is it?"

Agnes bobbed her head within the confines of the doorway for a moment longer and smiled. "I have brought something to inspire you all while you take your exam!"

My roomie sounded doubtful as he repeated the words of Soeur Marie, "What is it?"

Agnes could contain her excitement no longer. She entered the room and stood before us wearing an old (and worn) black gown. She appeared ecstatic as she informed us, "This is from the old days . . . from when I was a student." She lifted either side of the gown a few inches off the floor, smiled, and bowed.

George repeated, "What is it?"

Our instructress remained joyful. "It is my old graduation robe!" she said proudly. "I thought this would give each of you a little inspiration as you take your own final exam." She smiled once more and lifted the stylus from her desk. Suddenly, her appearance changed to one of seriousness; she waved the stylus before us. "It is time to cover the ground rules!"

She turned and wrote "Ground Rules" on the board and underlined the words twice over.

When she turned to face us, she said, "The exam is pass/fail." Then, the listing of rules began, "First, you will need to write your name on the top of the test. Second, I want to be very clear that there is to be no talking during this final! Third, keep your eyes on your own work; don't look at any test but your own."

She paused for only a moment to recall what came next, "Fourth, remain seated unless you are excused; if you want to be excused, raise your hand. Fifth, you absolutely may not refer to any notes or any pieces of paper other than the test I am giving you. Sixth, the first portion of the test will be essays—answer each question as completely as you can; the second portion is multiple choice. Seventh, you will have three hours to complete the final exam; if you finish early, you may leave once I excuse you."

After the rules had been covered, she asked, "Are there any questions?"

Only silence filled the room. I did not turn my head in either direction; instead, my gaze remained focused on the teacher before us. I could only assume that each of the others was doing the same. Agnes nodded in approval and began passing a stack of pages to each one of us. Once they were within my hand, I counted the pages before me . . . Twelve.

After writing my name at the top of the page, I glanced at the first question, "Part A: Provide and discuss three examples of how Hattie Jenning's time slip experience in Sevierville was different from the Moberly-Jourdan time slip. Part B: Provide and discuss three examples of how the Moberly-Jourdan time slip was similar to the Medieval time slip experience. Part C: How is the Liverpool time slip different than each of these other accounts?"

As soon as I had finished reading the question to myself, George mumbled aloud, "You have got to be kidding!"

Agnes slapped the top of her desk and reminded us, "There needs to be silence!"

It may be difficult to comprehend why some Wayfarers have chosen to abandon the League and the work to which we have dedicated ourselves. Although the question has long been considered by the Core, there may not be one solitary answer. Some have contended that a Work such as ours – one without seeming end, in pursuit of a goal that appears ever beyond reach – is fraught with weariness and fatigue. Others believe that the enticements of power and wealth are tempting to those who experienced lack within the illusion of space and time. There is a third explanation, however, that may prove to be the most accurate of all.

Although the Collective Illusion is nothing more than an illusory path of things that cannot ultimately be real, it is nonetheless a path that is known. It is a path that has long been experienced, recognized, and understood, whereas the path of the Prime Directive remains completely unknown. What shall be the experience of those who become part of it? What does such a path entail? When all of Creation is permeated with One Consciousness, what becomes of the Self? These questions cannot help but lead to some magnitude of apprehension and fear. And, ultimately, fear is the motivation that prompts some to remain in the familiar rather than choosing instead to move beyond themselves and experience the great unknown.

Excerpt, "Choosing Darkness or Choosing Light," *A Time Traveler's Code of Conduct* **by Ruth #7**

TEN: Journal Entry – December 6 ATL:

I have only enough time to make a quick note herein, as my day's schedule has suddenly taken the most surprising and delightful of turns. The change of plans is due to the fact that my sweetheart just announced we are going to celebrate my successful completion of Agnes's final exam (an accomplishment I will detail shortly). Apparently, we shall be undertaking the very adventure Athena described on the occasion of our first date. As I recall, we were alone in the café when she asserted the possibility of having a date experience "far from the League facility." I remember my surprise as she suggested, "We choose a place and time and look for a couple sharing a meal between them. They become our targets." Such a prospect has visited my thoughts on more than one occasion, for we will experience the sensations of the couple, as well as our own. Such an encounter is to be my "graduation present." The idea of the rendezvous has captivated me thoroughly.

In terms of the results of our examination, let me briefly describe the morning class period, as it offers yet another example of our instructress's desire to provide some semblance of theatrical component to our education.

I must admit feeling a measure of apprehension myself as we five gathered within the confines of the room for our normally scheduled class time. No doubt, it was an apprehension that was shared by us all. On the way, my roomie had even pondered aloud, "Why doesn't Agnes #23 just post our results on the door and be done with it?" To be sure, such an approach might have eliminated some of the nervousness that seemed to be evident on the faces of each of my classmates as they entered the classroom. Although we acknowledged one another with a brief nod or a glance, not a word was spoken between us as we took our seats. For her own part, in all manner of seriousness, Agnes paced back and forth before us keeping her eyes fixated upon the floor. To be sure, such a display may have lasted only a few minutes in duration but it felt far longer indeed.

Finally, Agnes stopped in place. She reached for the stylus on her desk, and began waving it before us, "It is time to announce the results of your final examination!" The proclamation nearly moved me to suggest that such an announcement might best be undertaken with each of us individually, but I confess that my own apprehension prevented such words from being spoken aloud. Like the others, I remained silent.

One at a time, Agnes passed back our examinations, declaring that she was doing so, "In alphabetical order!" As such, the next words she proclaimed became, "Ben #239, PASS!" She proceeded to drop the appropriate exam pages on the desk before me. Next came, "Bonne Soeur Marie #304, PASS!" who was handed her own examination, as well. "Emanuel #41, PASS!" followed. My roomie came next, "George #111, PASS!" And finally, "Manuela #64, PASS!" who was handed the twelve pages she had completed.

While the others were receiving their exams, I quickly glanced through the pages before me as a means of observing any notations that had been made to evaluate my responses. However, the only mark inscribed throughout the entire document was one word in capital letters on the first page, "PASS."

Agnes appeared to sigh with relief, and then waved the stylus before us, cheerfully announcing, "Congratulations! You all passed." However, her next words were spoken with some measure of severity, "I want to make it VERY CLEAR that when you start my graduate classes next semester, it will no longer be pass/fail!" She slapped her desk to emphasize the point, "You will need to achieve a score of at least 80 percent in order to pass!"

A moment later, she bobbed about and proclaimed with some measure of urgency, "As soon as possible, you need to go to the Recruitment Office and get your graduation robes from Nashwa! You will need to have everything in order before your graduation." Her final words were only, "Class dismissed!"

We five gathered in the hallway immediately after class to speak about our respective relief at having completed the curriculum. Each of us had passed the final exam! We were all to be Wayfarers! To be sure, there was some discussion between us as to whether our individual grasp of the material was most responsible for such an accomplishment, or whether Agnes's teaching proficiency itself was due some measure of credit. In the end, it was decided between us that the answer most likely contained an element of both.

I believe I surprised my sweetheart when I suggested Athens, Greece as the location of our planned adventure. When I expressed my city of choice, she appeared startled and quickly responded, "Are you certain you don't want to go to Paris or London, or even Philadelphia?" As I had spent sufficient time in each of the three locales, I assured her that I did not. My desire was to go to Greece, and who better to serve as a guide to such a place of beauty than my Athena?

The dining establishment she chose for our rendezvous was even more beautiful than I could have imagined. Not only did we have a view of the sparkling blue waters, but we were on the shoreline of the Marina itself, preparing to dine at a place that was apparently quite well known for its cuisine – the Moorings restaurant. The elegant couple we enveloped had been seated so that they possessed a panoramic view of our surroundings.

"You have truly outdone yourself, Athena!" I smiled and stared at her across the table as her ghostly form continued to surround the woman she had chosen as her target of influence. The woman went by the name Angeliki and appeared to be in possession of an abundance of wealth – four of her fingers were heavy with diamonds, a dazzling necklace hung around her neck, and her golden bracelet sparkled its reflection in the wine glasses upon the table before us.

"You know I adore you?" Athena replied as she twirled a strand of hair between her vaporous fingertips.

"I do," I said with a smile, "although I do not recall you mentioning that fact until this very moment."

She smiled in return, "I have been busy."

My own target was a businessman named Tobias, who possessed a deep tan and an apparent love for great quantities of cologne. From his own thoughts, I could discern that he was involved in the business of commercial shipping. In between sips of wine, he took occasion to make frequent comments to Angeliki regarding the various yachts and boats we could see within the harbor.

Athena waved her transparent hand at the menus before us, "We should decide what we want to eat before they do."

I was surprised, "We can choose?"

Athena answered with certainty, "As long as we pick something that they would eat, it won't be a problem. Just use your influence."

"That sounds wonderful!" I replied with some measure of joy. "Why haven't we done this sooner?"

My sweetheart turned loose of her hair and counted

off much that had been restrictive between us, "Let's see, your classes, my research, your mission assignments, my research, your reading and homework, my research . . . Shall I continue?"

I acquiesced, "That seems entirely sufficient to make the point."

I looked down in the direction of the menu just as Athena stated rather innocently, "I had a surprise visitor in the library today."

I looked up and inquired, "Really, who?"

Athena was to the point, "Louise #217 came to see me."

My eyes opened wide in alarm. "What?" was all that would come to mind.

Athena only nodded, "We talked a little about the work we were doing – hers in the ATL Mission Office and mine in the Akasha. She eventually inquired about you, and when I told her we were going on a date, she said you had something to ask me tonight. She was very mysterious about it, and would only say that it was something you wanted to ask me yourself." Athena looked me straight in the eyes, "What is it, Ben?"

I found myself stammering and very much certain that our evening adventure was about to come to an abrupt end. I finally managed, "I will tell you but these are not my words; they come from Louise."

My sweetheart said only, "I am listening."

With some measure of trepidation, I explained Louise's proposal. I also assured my sweetheart that I wanted to be with her. Afterward, Athena insisted that the three of us would be "meeting sometime tomorrow." In spite of the possibilities that had frequented my mind before the mention of Louise, afterward, I could think of little else but our planned confrontation. In the end, it was not my sweetheart who suggested we postpone our long-awaited adventure but me.

I inquired with concern, "What are we going to do?"

Athena replied, "Leave that to me. I need to do some research."

"Are you certain this needs to be done tomorrow?"

My sweetheart was most certain, "Yes."

Shortly thereafter, we departed the presence of Tobias and Angeliki and returned to the League. There was to be no dinner adventure that evening, and it was a certainty there would be no shaking of the sheets. Although Athena did promise we would soon revisit the Moorings restaurant after her research and our prescribed confrontation had taken place, I stopped thinking about the adventure and turned instead to the meeting between the three of us. Just as the anticipation of Agnes's final exam had given me a sufficient measure of apprehension, the sense of foreboding regarding the discussion felt very much the same.

The next afternoon, Athena and I sat at one of the tables in the Akasha Library, waiting for Louise to arrive. My sweetheart had sent a message to the ATL Mission Office informing Louise that it was time for the three of us to meet. One of the Akasha volumes had been placed on the table before us, as was a folder with several pieces of paper tucked inside.

When I inquired about the material Athena had gathered for our discussion, she would say only, "You will see shortly."

When I requested some measure of outline regarding

the conversation that was to occur between us so that I might be sufficiently prepared, she replied, "I am going to do most of the talking."

To my surprise, Athena appeared quite calm. She held a few strands of dark hair between her fingertips, twirling them in quiet contemplation as though deep in thought. I said no more and waited. It was not long before the dreaded moment arrived.

I rose to greet Louise as she approached the table. Even on this occasion, I could not help but notice her blonde hair and her sparkling blue eyes. Athena motioned for her to sit across from us but remained seated herself.

Louise took her seat. She, too, appeared to possess no measure of nervousness. In truth, she seemed rather joyful, "My dearest friends," she said with her French accent, "I am so very pleased we can have this conversation together!"

Athena was quick to reply, "We *need* to have this conversation. I want to be completely honest and upfront, Louise." She looked Louise straight in the eyes, "The three of us are not going to have a relationship. We are not going to have a throuple. There will be no ménage à trois."

Louise was undeterred, "Perhaps we should vote on the matter? I would love to hear Ben's thoughts on the idea."

Athena turned toward me, "Ben, please tell Louise what you told me last night. Who do you want to be with?"

Before I could speak a word, Louise interjected, "Ben, if Athena is not interested in satisfying the connection we feel between us, perhaps you and I could be together?"

I was quick to assert, "Athena is my sweetheart. I want to be with her."

Louise sighed, reaching across the table to gently stroke

the side of my face, "Do you not find me attractive?"

I used my hand to remove her fingers from my face, placing her hand back on the tabletop, "Please, Louise, I want to be with Athena."

"We shall see, my Ben," Louise said assuredly. "We shall see."

Finally, Athena had had enough. "Okay, Louise, let me tell you what I know." She tapped the top of the Akasha volume as Louise turned to look in her direction. "I did some research and found that before your recruitment, you spent many, many years alone."

Louise was quick to respond, "I did not. I was married!"

"True," Athena admitted, "but your husband was so absorbed with his work, you felt abandoned much of the time. You told those closest to you that his obsession caused you to believe he was 'out of his mind.' He could think of little else. According to the records, there was very little time spent between you."

Louise was silent.

Athena took the folder upon the table between her hands, and continued, "His name was Louis Daguerre . . ."

I interrupted, "The name is unfamiliar to me."

"He invented the Daguerreotype," she said quickly. My look of confusion prompted her to repeat the word in syllables, "Da-ger-a-type," she said. "It was an early form of photography in the 1830s in France."

To my surprise, the words prompted Louise to look nervously at Athena's folder. My sweetheart continued, "Ben, whenever you feel drawn to Louise's beauty, I want you to remember this." She passed the folder to me.

I took it between my hands, opened it, and was startled to see a stark photograph of an elderly woman who appeared much oppressed by the challenges of life. Her face was worn and wrinkled without any semblance of joy whatsoever. Her lips formed a frown. Her hair was unkempt and frazzled, aside from an uneven line that parted it in the middle. She held her head upon one hand and stared out from the picture with both sadness and distress. I turned aside the photograph to gaze upon the next, only to find it was much the same as the one that had come before. I set the second photo aside, discovering another image of the same, miserable woman staring out at me. Each of the three images appeared as unhappy as the last.

"Who is this poor woman?" I voiced with concern.

Athena replied, "She was the subject of several of Daguerre's photos. Her name is Louise Georgina Smith, and she was married to him. Isn't that right, Louise?"

Louise lowered her head and pulled her hands back from the tabletop, "What do you want?"

Athena's first words were spoken with severity, "You need to stop pursuing Ben." What came next was more congenial, "Louise, we can be friends, but I want to be clear . . . Ben wants to be with me."

As though deep in thought, Louise was silent for only a moment. She appeared to ponder the situation and then turned to look at us both, nodded in agreement, and said finally, "Friendship between us will be fine . . ." She added with a smile, "Perhaps it would be appropriate for me to give consideration to George or Emanuel?"

The day of our long-awaited graduation had arrived at last. Following Agnes's instruction, my classmates and I had already acquired our graduation gowns from the Recruitment Office. The celebration was to be held within the central chamber of the Akasha Library, followed by a special banquet repast in the League Café. By all accounts, these graduation festivities were taken quite seriously by the Core.

"I heard all members of the Core – all nine! – are usually present for the occasion," George informed me as we dressed within our chambers.

I nodded and informed him, "Athena tells me that as part of the ceremony all graduates are given their first assignment as official Wayfarers."

My roomie's retort was quick, "You have got to be kidding! Doesn't anyone around here know about a day off?"

I understood his frustration, prompting my response, "It would seem that within this profession leisure is not of utmost importance. Athena and I have yet to schedule our dinner adventure."

George looked at me most seriously, "Is everything okay between you two . . . and Louise?"

My reply sounded certain, "It seems so," before inquiring, "And how are things with *you* and Louise?"

He appeared confused, "I have not seen her."

"Give it time," I mouthed only to myself.

Once we were appropriately attired and had assured one another that our appearance was sufficiently proper for the occasion before us, we made our way to the Akasha Library. Other than a few words of observation, our minds seemed occupied with thoughts of what lay before us. Little was spoken during the journey, and the trip itself seemed much swifter than usual.

When we arrived at the double doorways and entered the chamber, we were greeted by the sounds of more voices and chatter than was appropriate for a library. People gathered throughout the central chamber (a few I had never seen), and nearly 40 chairs had been arranged in front of the podium. A large banner had been taped behind the lectern, "Congratulations, Graduates!" On top of the podium, I could see five rolled diplomas, each tied with a ribbon.

Elder Professor Grimwald was sitting in the back row next to Ruth #7. Emma #119 was standing on the other side of the row frowning with irritation. My roomie and I began walking toward the front, passing Louise who said only, "Hello, Ben," before adding with a warm smile, "Nice to see you, George." Although appearing somewhat surprised by her greeting, my roomie quickly responded, and soon thereafter we made our way to the front row where a long ribbon (emblazoned with "Saved for Graduates") had been placed over five chairs.

In the midst of friendly greetings and ongoing conversations, all those present began to take a seat. After leaning forward to place a kiss upon my cheek, Athena sat in the row behind us. Emanuel, Manuela, and Soeur Marie soon took their seats next to us. I turned to see Hina #407 (the woman from Grimwald's original recruitment class) walking next to Hakim #60, who towered above her. Three chairs had been placed beside the podium and were soon filled with Sara #11, Milton #71, and Agnes #23, our graduate speakers.

With the appearance of Agnes, George turned to me and said with a smile, "I sure hope she has some background information for us."

The remaining members of the Core arrived together (Lucius #19, Mia #161, and Nashwa #86), each taking a chair near Grimwald. The conversations throughout the chamber continued until Milton #71 moved toward the podium and stood waiting for all to become quiet. When the crowd was finally silent, Milton stated cheerfully, "Welcome to this most magnificent occasion! The graduation of our newest Wayfarers."

The sound of applause erupted through the room (from what I observed no one was clapping more enthusiastically than Agnes herself). During the clapping, I felt Athena squeeze my shoulders from behind. The applause went on and on for quite some time. When it was over, Milton thanked all those present for coming to the occasion. He then added his own appreciation of the graduates, "I want to say that the ATL Mission Office is truly grateful for all those mission assignments that our graduating class has already undertaken successfully. They have been a tremendous help to our work!" He led us through another round of applause before introducing Sara #11 as "our beloved Governor-General."

Sara came forward and began. "On behalf of the Core, I want to thank Ben #239, Bonne Soeur Marie #304, Emanuel #41, George #111, and Manuela #64 for their dedication." As our names were spoken aloud, Sara looked at each of us individually. "Since the very beginning of the League, only a few have committed themselves to undertake all that is necessary to become a part of this work. Thank you for your service! What we do is not easy. It seldom brings accolades or rewards, but it can be fulfilling. For myself, I find it especially rewarding when I have the opportunity to work with individuals like you five who are graduating today."

There was a few scattered applause before she continued, "One at a time, I will call each of our graduates by name, and tell you a little about them." Sara turned again to look at us, "After your name is called, please come forward, listen to what I have to say, and then accept your diploma." She turned back to the audience, "Once the diplomas have been distributed, Agnes #23 will announce the first mission assignments that each of our new Wayfarer Time Travelers will be undertaking shortly." The Governor-General nodded in approval, concluding with, "After the missions have been announced, you will be dismissed, and we will immediately reconvene in the League Café for a celebratory banquet!"

Sara began with me, "Ben #239." I stood and moved toward the podium as she proceeded to highlight my commitment to diplomacy. When she had finished her remarks, Milton passed me a diploma. Bonne Soeur Marie came next and was praised for her own work with healing. For Emanuel, we heard of his dedication to transformation and personal spirituality. George was extolled as a "most dedicated philanthropist." Finally, Manuela was commended for her commitment to equality and her work with the underprivileged. Once again, Sara congratulated the five of us, and there was another round of applause.

Agnes #23 came to the podium and smiled proudly, "It is my honor and privilege to announce these mission assignments for our newest Wayfarers." She pulled a folded piece of paper from her pocket, unfolded it before us, and began reading:

"Ben #239, destination Washington, DC, 1941, in the matter of Eleanor Roosevelt, and her destiny as global ambassador."

"Bonne Soeur Marie #304, destination London, King's College, 2054, in the matter of the eradication of cancer."

"Emanuel #41, destination Vatican City, 2123, in the matter of the reunification of Eastern Orthodoxy and Catholicism."

"George #111, destination the Philippines, 2020, in the matter of philanthropic endeavors to address a coronavirus."

"Manuela #64, destination Babylon, 539 BC, in the

matter of Cyrus the Great, and the emancipation of slaves." Agnes began bobbing about as she said, "You are now officially Wayfarers – members of the Time Travel profession. Congratulations!" When her words had been spoken, there was some manner of commotion at the back of the chamber. Voices began rising above one another, prompting those seated to turn to see what was occurring. Agnes glanced in the direction of the disturbance just as I turned to see what was happening. A moment later, Agnes yelled in distress, "It's Gregory!" She sounded horrified, "He's supposed to be eradicated!"

All eyes in the room turned to face Gregory #143. He stood before us and spoke loud enough for all those present to hear, "Ruth, as you requested of me, I found Emmett! I know the timeline he is altering."

After Gregory's arrival and his surprising announcement, noise, commotion and disorder came from every direction. Many of those present ran forward to speak with Gregory himself. Members of the Core gathered around Ruth #7 to hear what she had to say. For our own part, George and I turned to Athena, confessing the secret Ruth had insisted we hold in complete confidence.

"We swore we would not even speak of it between us," I admitted to Athena. "It was part of Ruth's plan to find Emmett."

Athena looked bewildered, "Instead of eradicating Gregory, she asked him to find Emmett?"

"She did," my roomie was quick to reply. "She told Gregory to revisit occasions within his own timeline, waiting for Emmett to find him. Once that occurred, he was to join Emmett and discover the alternate timeline." George added, "Ruth knows how Emmett thinks better than anyone."

After those present had gained some semblance of understanding as to the course of events Ruth had put into motion, there was much confusion as to what would come next. Some pondered aloud when, and if, Gregory #143 would be returned to one hour after his recruitment – Agnes was among them. Several members of the Core suggested that a journey to apprehend Emmett needed to be undertaken immediately. Others insisted that such an assignment required much more planning and should wait for the Core to properly prepare. I heard one of the café staff ask Milton whether they should postpone the banquet. In the end, the Governor-General herself made the announcement.

"My dear friends," she declared from the podium once the chamber had become sufficiently quiet, "we will continue with our planned graduation activities. We will deal with this latest announcement as soon as we are able."

For that reason, within the hour we gathered in the League Café for the celebratory meal that had been prepared for the graduating class. I was quite pleased to find sliced turkey and cranberries among the options. I followed Athena with my plate in hand to a table where we could sit with my classmates. Bonne Soeur Marie and Manuela had both selected the fish and rice. Emanuel had chosen his usual fare of vegetables and rolls, and George had some manner of curry on the platter before him. I made note of the fact that Louise #217 was speaking to both of them as the three moved toward the table together and sat across from my sweetheart and me. I nudged Athena's arm, whispering only, "Look at that."

The evening proved to be one of conversation and leisure. We ate, talked, and laughed amongst ourselves at the various memories we shared of Agnes's curriculum. It had truly been a journey for each of us – not one soon to be forgotten. In between mouthfuls and dialogue, I made note of those present. I saw Agnes and Nashwa sitting with Elder Professor Grimwald and Hakim – even as he sat, he towered about the three. I perceived Ruth and Gregory sitting alone by themselves, causing me to wonder whether they discussed the subject of eradication or instead Gregory's possible return to the League. I found Sara sitting with three other members of the Core: Mia, Lucius, and Hina. And I made note of how the sounds of laughter, joy, and camaraderie filled the room. On such an occasion, it was good to be a Time Traveler.

Suddenly, George looked at me from across the table, "Have you seen Milton?" he inquired aloud.

I pondered the query for only a moment before admitting that I had not, "I wonder where he is?"

It was Louise who pointed toward the doorway and announced, "He is right there."

I turned to see our ATL Mission Supervisor enter the café; his face filled with alarm. His distressed appearance brought much of the conversation within the room to a complete stop. The Governor-General rose to greet him just as he yelled, "Emma #119 has been taken."

Later that evening, I bid goodnight to Athena, and quickly returned to my chambers to join with my roomie in what was to come. It had been announced that our mission was to leave immediately. At that very moment, Sara #11, Milton #71, and Ruth #7 were gathered with the Core to discuss the final details of our planned assault. Together, we would find Emmett, retrieve Emma, and bring the alternate timeline to a halt once and for all. Although I was uncertain who from the Core would be joining us, it had already been requested that all five graduates take part in the assignment.

When I opened the door, George was standing there, waiting for me.

He smiled, lifted his Horologium in hand, and asked, "Are you ready to find some rebel Time Travelers?"

A Note to Readers:

Many aspects of the historical incidents detailed within *A Time Traveler's Commencement* are true, including the invention of the daguerreotype by Louis Daguerre and his marriage to Louise Georgina Smith. For those who are interested, the Hamburg bombing time slip, the Abbeville time slip, and the Liverpool time slip can all be Googled for additional information.

In regard to the Sevierville time slip, this story was told to me personally by the woman who experienced it firsthand. Her only request was that I not reveal her real name. For that reason, she is known within these pages as Hattie Jennings.

Made in United States
Orlando, FL
16 January 2024

42585495R00115